MARC
A.M. HOUNCHELL

QUINTESSENTIAL
Reality

MARC D. CREPEAUX & A.M. HOUNCHELL

QUINTESSENTIAL REALITY

First Printing, 2018

Rusty Wheels Media, LLC.
P.O. Box 1692
Rome, GA 30162

ISBN-13: 978-0692094846

ISBN-10: 0692094849

Printed in the United States of America

RUSTY WHEELS MEDIA
THEY KEEP TURNING

MARC D. CREPEAUX & A.M. HOUNCHELL

QUINTESSENTIAL REALITY

MARC D. CREPEAUX & A.M. HOUNCHELL

To those who suffer both the curse and blessing of mental illness.

-Marc

To Mrs. Switzer who taught me to grip my insanity and bleed it onto paper.

-A.M.

For projects past, and this precious book. Let there be many more in our future...

-Marc, RWM

MARC D. CREPEAUX & A.M. HOUNCHELL

CHAPTER One

Drowning in an era of time and dreams, Shelly awoke with a rush of anticipation. She tossed off her sheets, thrilled to meet her new destiny.

Automatic lights went out and the percussive cadence of sprinklers erupted throughout the cul-de-sac. The oncoming sun tried to make up for being tardy as daylight savings time occurred only a few weeks prior. Birds were weary of this late hour too, as they were eager to dig worms which rose from the newfound life. This water penetrated the skin of the earth and its silver-green grass.

The sun emptied shadows all across the neighborhood until the almost white pavement sparkled with the minerals found in the region's soil. This sparkle would later cause the need for some to don sunglasses, less they feel enchanted by the false sense of summer.

While only in the low fifties at this early morning, the eager sun would eventually rise to the high seventies and risk a glimpse at what was surely to come as the season went on, terrible humidity. This would cause all in the neighborhood to switch on their central air units a bit early, just here and there, in order to cut through the soon to be an impenetrable, moisture-laden heat monster.

All along the uniform pavement, gutters emptied near planned trees while electric transfer boxes and tip-top fire hydrants held down the fort. Shadows were evacuated from their comfortable positions. This Saturday morning proved that not all people were ready to accept the *modern* tradition of advancing their hands on the clock.

There were some who took advantage of the listlessness of others. These ambitious souls squirted water which led into bubbled streams at the end of their perfect driveways. With stamped house numbers intact in the cement, they washed their cars and trucks, soaping away the weekly commutes to nowhere.

Maybe one in eight of the uniformed houses in the long, hilly rows of the sought-after *Nottingham Estates* subdivision showed signs of life. A father or dog was sent out to fetch a paper only to go right back in. This led to a state of wondering who had yet to stir in this house or that.

The eager paperboy of the neighborhood, Tommy Sanders, was late by the clocks, but not by the sun. He pedaled with urgency that lacked a frantic sense as he gracefully threw each paper, coated with thin plastic sleeve, on, or at least near, the front porches. The same way his older brother had taught him.

For those who still read news the old fashioned way, these headlines only served as a mirage of weak subtlety in this, the most perfect existence. Surely, any bad news contained within the black and white of Tommy's papers would offer cheap talk amongst tea pals or a grunt of recognition to neighbors between passes. Nothing bad in those pages would touch anyone here.

Not all the news that Tommy threw on yards, walkways, and the occasional porch was negative, or black and white either. Celebrations, advertisements, announcements, and the occasional estate sale were all prized after.

As Tommy whizzed by 2140 Archer Court on his Mongoose, he threw a paper that landed just to the right of a walkway, half-on, half-off the perfect, shimmering Bermuda grass.

This paper contained in the upper right-hand corner a picture of a house and the stunning headshot of its new seller, a Michelle "Shelly" Dougherty, the new proprietor of *Quintessential Realty Co.*

When the boy pedaled on, the heavy, custom-built

front door with the golden pegged letters *2140* burst open, revealing a waiting Shelly Dougherty in her pink bathrobe and slippers. The tall, slender, beautiful woman of about forty was clearly busying herself with preparations of her body. Her auburn hair was in the most modern curl set, ready to poof up her day. Her nails were perfect, a dark, velvet-red with high gloss. The nails snatched the paper as her already shadowed eyes with tasteful mascara glanced about the neighborhood. No one saw her when she peered around. She smiled. Her lipstick was not a part of the preparation just yet. Shelly darted back inside, slammed the door, and tore the plastic sheath from her masterpiece.

She giggled to nobody as she saw the front inset which gave a preview of her half page ad. That ad nearly cost her a thousand dollars. She eagerly separated the pages inside, tore past the comics, and found it under the weather.

"Under the weather even!" she cried out to an empty stairwell. She saw her big *Q* logo for *Quintessential*. So big, so bold, and so artistic. She worked on it with a graphic designer for months, had seen it on her signs, and already on her new business cards. Now it was all the more real, all the more out in the open.

She saw her own photo and held her breath. The business woman turned her head to match the pose in the photo, clenched her teach in uncertainty, and tapped her foot. Then, she moved her eyes to the house, 68 Maple

Grove.

The photos of the advertised mansion were marvelous. A modern Tudor like this was deep, yet edgy. The ad showcased every sharp corner on the roof, the splendor of the expensive landscaping, and every other feature Shelly knew would draw attention to the five-bedroom, four-bathroom mint of a home that cost only six hundred thousand. There were another four houses listed at lower prices closer to a quarter million, but today was the debut of Maple Grove. Today was the open house, her very own open house. Today was her debut.

Shelly worked for a handful of real estate companies in the area but soon grew tired of showing *handyman specials* and the ever-present foreclosure or short-sale. Those transactions weren't short at all. She wanted high-end. She wanted to dazzle and surprise eager buyers who wouldn't quibble over a few thousand dollars or a needed repair. She wanted big commissions too, and she started to get them at the end of her last stint at Holloway Realty.

Shelly had been groomed for the more expensive properties by none other than Mr. Holloway himself. He showed her how to seal the endgame tight on a number of high dollar dreams. She tasted the fine dining that was necessary to make real deals. She acclimated herself to the common appearances of that upper-upper middle class of buyers that would just about do. She bought a Mercedes. Her wardrobe received an upgrade and she wore only real jewelry that shined as much as her smile.

In the end, she needed a way out of Holloway Realty. Mr. Holloway was retiring to golf and his slime ball son, Frank, was taking over. Shelly didn't get along with Frank. He made a pass at her despite her gaudy wedding ring. She had said *no thanks*, and he grew cold and disagreeable. He would shoot down even the smallest of observations that Shelly would offer at meetings during the transition.

That was when the ideas began to surface for her own operation. Shelly knew that Quintessential Realty would be difficult at first, and that it would take a considerable amount of capital investment. Luckily, she had been rolling in the high-dollar commissions which she avoided getting taxed on by starting her own firm.

Also, her husband Andrew made good money as a software engineer, much more than her, for now. Andrew was willing to support her desires and ambitions as well as pick up any slack with the kids, something he had been doing more and more anyway.

Their two children, Andy and Julia, were twelve and fifteen. The younger boy had baseball games, scouts, swimming, and trumpet lessons which her husband usually tended to on the weekdays and weekends, when Shelly had been showing houses. Their daughter was self-sufficient most of the time, needing rides every so often but she mostly asked for money. Julia, who refused to be called *Julie*, after her mother's ending, grew somewhat fitful as she developed. This revealed a natural touch of hatred for her mother.

Julia was popular for her age, but not yet popular enough to warrant the attention of senior boys which pleased her father. She was involved in many extracurricular activities but complained and praised most about the school newspaper. She aimed to be editor *before* she was a senior and regaled her family often, regarding the dramatic power plays that were involved in achieving her end. Shelly hardly ever read her writing, but in that too, Andrew was there. He often took up the charge and pencil-marked her drafts.

Shelly stood there in the foyer of her silent house, carefully clutching the newspaper. Everyone was still asleep, but she wanted to show someone her ad. Andrew needed his rest and the kids were not likely to care, especially Julia, so Shelly made for the kitchen to fetch some scissors.

She carefully cut out her ad and front inset and presented them neatly on the fridge with a handful of magnets. It looked less impressive, backed by the sharp steel, but she made a mental note to buy a nice frame for her new office later.

With that in check, Shelly whirled around and noted the time on the matching microwave oven. 8AM, which meant she had exactly two hours to eat a Greek yogurt, get dressed, kiss Andy before his baseball game, and get over to Maple Grove for the rest of the preparations that remained from the night before.

Depending on how long the open house took, she would rush over to Andy's last few innings, answer any missed phone calls on the way home, and celebrate by the neighborhood's clubhouse pool with Nina, her closest friend. That evening, Nina's husband would grill steak and chicken with Andrew, the kids would swim, and she could celebrate her first performance.

There, all set.

Shelly knew what had to be done to get there. After that? Who knows? Maybe Andrew would get a little horny from the imported beers, the swimming, and the steak. She would get a celebratory lay that evening.

With that naughty thought, Shelly opened the fridge. She grabbed again with her nails, and popped open her much needed breakfast. After, she tiptoed for the last leg of her morning routine about the bathroom and the walk-in closet. Shelly aimed to tell Andrew goodbye with a morning kiss and a *wish me luck*, but all she got was a groan from her sleeping husband. She did not see anyone else before leaving, and forgot to kiss little Andy before baseball. Still, the professional in her remained armed with the goals of the day.

Shelly was purposeful and alone.

I was stealing from something that could need it. Everything in the suburb needed water. The neighbor's

lawn, my lawn, the bright red Lambo. We are toxic green cacti soaking up water in the concrete desert. Even when everything was covered in water, and I glanced out to my front lawn, the light was so bright. It bounced from the sidewalk like patches of snow. This place was a robot version of the Garden of Eden.

Several rectangles arranged in different rectangular patterns, colored the same, machine pressed like clock parts. Yet, time still went on. Time ticked on by. Getting older, and we would continue to do so in paradise.

My time was spread unevenly between obligations. I was finally getting my big break. A six-hundred thousand dollar house. It was larger than my own, but I didn't need five bedrooms and four bathrooms. I was hardly convinced that anyone did. At the very least, the home was proper.

All I wanted was to move from this tiny fish in the artificial pond to a big fish somewhere, anywhere. Make more money than Andrew. He never lorded it over me, but I wanted to make more, so much more.

I tiptoed to the fridge, careful to avoid the minefield of squeaky boards yet to fix. After three years, I figured that it would be easier to just avoid them. Too early to cook breakfast, so I grabbed a Greek yogurt and snapped it open; blueberry. I tore through it, hungry like a lioness. Today was my day. Today WAS my day.

I tossed the yogurt in the trash, making a mental note

of its fullness. Julie had left a note pinned to the fridge. It was another message, asking for money like it always was. Was she not aware of how close my bedroom was to hers? Was she not?

I wasn't going to let her break me. Not on My Day. If she wanted money from me, she could come get it, face-to-face. Or, she could do without.

The last leg of my morning strut was back in my room. I got dressed, watching Andy lightly snoring. I kissed him, but he didn't say anything. Fine. I just continued the Quintessential motto.

It is My Day.

CHAPTER Two

When Shelly arrived at the Maple Grove property, she looked in her backseat at the balloons, frowned, and decided to leave them there. They were far too tacky for this kind of sale, even though they did match the color scheme of the house perfectly. She made sure of that when she ordered them. She opened her trunk and almost giggled but tried to remain calm. In it were her new signs, finished over a week ago. One for the corner, one for the front which would remain until the house sold. With any luck on her side, that realization could be as soon as today. Shelly composed herself and removed the signs and stuck them in the ground with her small hammer. She was careful not to get her dress dirty.

Inside, she filled the silver ice bucket with the bags. She positioned the *Perrier* sparkling water just so in the foyer along with her cards and printouts of the house. She placed the hors d'oeuvres from Whole Foods in the kitchen, but not obtrusively, along with another silver ice bucket with bottled water on the granite counter.

Shelly then ran out of things to do. Most everything else had been done the night before. The pool was ready, the grounds were ready, and the furniture was staged at a high price a few days prior. She decided to do a walk through with some rehearsal one last time. She glanced at her phone, thirty minutes to go.

"Welcome, welcome!" she said, standing at a pivot from the invisible buyers. That way, they could see all the custom design and high ceilings right away. They could witness the breathtaking entrance from the start. She learned this a long time ago. As she made her way around the house, she explained features and expensive niceties.

By the time she got upstairs, she had it all down and discontinued the vocalization of her lines. By then, she would either have them, or she wouldn't. The house would sell itself. She only had to be convincing enough to get out of the way of a potential sale and to maintain its high price. She learned these tricks a long time ago.

Still, when she found herself back in the kitchen, her feet began to pace on the marble floor. This occurred at a faster pace as she looked at her phone. It was five after the hour and no one was there to see the house yet. Not even nosy neighbors, not even another real estate agent.

Shelly paced on and waited for the chimed doorbell to ring. She needed the assurance that what she was doing was right, that going out on her own had been a good move. She needed to know that the market was picking back up and focusing on high-end properties would lighten her work load and fatten her wallet. She needed to know this would work.

After twenty-two more minutes of excruciating doubt, the doorbell rang and she rushed out of the kitchen. The businesswoman composed herself by the door before opening with her biggest smile and most delightful greeting.

The first couple to see the house was a doctor and his wife who were planning a move from Winnipeg. She appeared to be white, while the doctor could have been Indian or Middle Eastern. Shelly pretended to know where Winnipeg was and didn't blink an eye when the doctor mentioned his specialty. She simply didn't know what those types of doctors did.

Regardless, Shelly pulled the tour off, even cozied up to the woman as she was shown, and remained very respectful in answering the doctor's many questions. Even though Shelly was a pro, she felt it necessary to go back to the basics with the opening of her own business. The couple just got into town, picked up a paper at the coffee shop, and rushed right over to see the house.

Once the tour was complete, the three found themselves upstairs on the veranda. Shelly always felt awkward in these moments, though it hardly ever showed.

Luckily, the good doctor spoke up first, "And the asking price is six-hundred thousand, correct?" The olive-skinned doctor kept asking his questions with a tone of confirmation at the end.

"Correct," Shelly answered without a sense of wanting to haggle or pretend to give inside information just yet.

"And I assume you have the inspection?" he asked, the woman had already whispered in his ear and pointed around the house with a beaming smile a number of times throughout the tour. This was a good sign for Shelly.

"Yes, everything is in order. I have all the documentation downstairs if you like."

"Not now, later. I have a meeting to get to this afternoon but... we'll take the house."

"You'll what?" Shelly stopped herself on the last word, careful not to act shocked. This was the big leagues and this was her first game. "Oh, I am so pleased that you like this home." That was all she could say.

The man gazed bleary-eyed at his wife, the crown moldings, the fixtures, the bannister, then back at his wife. "This is the house we have dreamed of for so long" he said, almost swallowing his words.

This took Shelly back. The man had been so curt,

coarse even throughout the tour. He acted like he didn't like swimming when she mentioned the pool. Yet here he was, almost to tears at the top of the stairs.

"Six hundred thousand will be just fine" he said, gaining his composure.

At this, Shelly nearly looked for the hidden cameras. It should never be this easy and she was about to ask for information regarding the finances when the doctor chimed in.

"We'll have our attorney call with the purchase offer and proof of finances on Monday morning" he said, holding her card way out in front. He forgot his bifocals.

"Great! That would be wonderful. I know you are going to be so happy in this house!" Shelly stammered at that, she didn't know what to do next. She would either pass out on the banister or float down the steps but she was saved once again. The doorbell rang. "Oh, ah…"

"Best that we run along for now, my appointment waits. Don't forget, Monday morning, first thing. He will call and we will get it all settled." The husband and wife made for the stairs and Shelly followed.

At the door, Shelly forgot all about the basics with the next couple and the next. She ignored the subtleties of the dance between agent and prospective buyer all throughout the following six tours. No one offered to buy then and there, but that was a good showing. A great first day for anybody with a high-priced estate in any location.

She remarked on this success alone as she drove away in her car. When she backed out of the long driveway in her Mercedes, she stopped at the end and marveled at the sign. Her sign and the artistic *Q*.

She knew they wouldn't all be like this, but this was one heck of a start. As she was driving to her son's baseball game, she tried to call Andrew, but that didn't work. He was probably cheering on the batters.

The prideful businesswoman nearly ran off the road after receiving an email from an attorney in Winnipeg. The attachment, which she had to pull over to retrieve, showed a preapproval letter for the first couple at *1.2 million dollars*.

She put the car into park to stop herself from slamming on something. Shelly couldn't believe her eyes. No wonder the couple didn't haggle, they had the buying power of twice that of Maple Grove. Shelly laughed so loud and whooped for good measure at her new-found success and fortune.

With this start, anything was possible. On this early Saturday afternoon, her life was full of real, verified purpose. She drove slowly and carefully, so as not to jinx her luck, as she found her way to her son's baseball game. Who knows, Shelly could even catch a few extra innings.

The motto changed a bit as I chanted welcomes. It was hard to nail down the correct level of assertiveness and willingness to please.

"Welcome!"

"Welcome."

"Welcome?"

None of them sounded quite right, so I rearranged everything meticulously. I moved the small world until it looked like a painting.

Another twenty minutes and still no one had arrived. I was running out of ways to flourish nine bottles of water. It would make sense for no one to show up. It was my first open house. No one knew about me or Quintessential Realty. My ad was simple.

The doorbell rang. Beyond the solid door was the first couple of people to see the property. It was a white woman and an Indian Doctor from a place that I had neither heard of, nor cared to look up. It didn't matter to me, I just smiled and nodded. It was perhaps the only thing I had in my arsenal.

They had a near unbelievable story.

It didn't show in his voice. He asked questions like someone who knew about architecture. I did my spins, quick laughs, I answered questions as quickly as I could.

I always detested the people who wouldn't stop asking questions, even when I was in the middle of a presentation. She had the mentality of someone who got whatever they wanted. The doctor was her gold mine, and she knew how to squeeze him for everything he was worth.

Once I finished up, we found ourselves downstairs in a brief moment of silence.

I expected him to say that they would think about it, or that he would think it over. It was always something along those lines. People who knew big words liked to talk big game and that never panned out. That wasn't what happened.

The Doctor glanced to the aspects of the house that weren't on point and then back to his wife. She nodded slightly, as I expected before. Gold digger. It was unsettling, but it worked for me. He said the thing they all say about the house being the one that they've dreamed.

I looked into the corners of the room for hidden cameras, even though I'd been there all week. The next words he said were a blur. Everything was coated in victory, even as I let them go back into the green of the concrete wasteland. I was transfixed, even as I showed the house to the next six couples. None of them looked like they had money.

The offer was extremely firm.

When I finally got to shut the door on the final couple, I danced. It had been my day. A roar escaped my mouth, but I let it continue. I was a proud lioness.

I couldn't wait to get home and hold it above Andrew's head. Maybe then, he'd look at me with lust in his eyes. On my way out, I glanced back at the Q on my sign. It was the answer to all of my questions. An artistic expression of my innermost desire. It was Quintessential, really.

I had to stop the car to keep from driving off the road.

MARC D. CREPEAUX & A.M. HOUNCHELL

CHAPTER Three

Shelly rolled over the hot pavement and saw a number of creative parking jobs. The drivers must have had no regard for *after the game*. The exits would be at a standstill. She found her husband's Nissan Xterra and sidled up parallel to his doors. She figured that if the need was there to park anybody in with her coup, it would have to be him.

Shelly could not see the ball field as she exited her car. She could see other uniforms, but not Andy's Bandits' colors. Families were going to and from the uplifted field area. As she crested the small hill by way of the stairs, Shelly realized that there was not one, but several baseball games going on at the same complex. The game in front of her was a T-ball variety, and it was just getting started with whining, confusion, and excitement.

She spun around on her flats, making sure that she did block the right blue Nissan. The strange zombie family stickers that she told her husband she hated was in the lower left, right where she always saw them in the garage. She checked her phone, no missed calls or texts, no unopened emails. Check. Then she started texting her husband for the correct field as she marched past the busy moms and dads in their shorts and tennis shoes. She nearly ran into one couple holding a little sport by both arms and suddenly felt out of place.

Shelly stopped mid-text and called her husband again. No answer. She looked down at her clothes and wished that she had changed out of her suit and flats. It was getting hot and she wondered just how many fields there were and how far the current path her overdressed shoes would take her.

As she continued the dodgy march, about to try her husband again, she heard a loud roar rom two stadiums beyond. Shelly put her phone away and decided that had to be the game she was supposed to see.

As she approached the louder ballfield, she could make out the little crowd of her son's team jerseys. The red contrasted with sleek, silver lettering of the *Bandits* caught her eye. What commanded her attention next was her husband whooping for little Andy. Just about the whole crowd was on their feet cheering at something. Shelly paused in a moment of longing as she watched her handsome husband and their smiling baby caught in a moment of boyish love.

Andrew saw her too and waved her in like a goofy, excited composer. Shelly didn't know what to do at first, as she was on the wrong side of the dugout. She tiptoed along the backstop as the old pitcher from the opposing team was relieved and the new one warmed up. A wild ball from the cold pitcher hit the fence as she walked by. Shelly gave a little squeal and ran.

"Mommy! I hit a home run!" Andy declared, his smile beaming in the sunshine. He held out his arms for a celebratory hug.

"Oh, that's great Andy! All that practice with your father in the back yard. How far did it go?" Shelly asked, giving Andy a big squeeze then looking out beyond the field.

"Far enough to bring two runners in and get that pitcher off the mound," her husband said with that same giddy smile, giving her a peck on the cheek. He knelt down to the boy. "Now Andy, there's three innings left. If you get up again, keep your eye on the ball…"

"And put the bat where the ball is. Got it dad!" Andy scooted back to his place on the bench, receiving more high fives from his teammates. Most of them were bigger in size, but not as good of a short stop, and not always the best hitters. That's because they didn't have Andrew Dougherty as their father, and they all somehow knew it.

"What's the score?" Shelly asked, searching for the digital board.

"7-3 and we're winning. They're bringing in a new pitcher now, but we got them beat," Andrew munched popcorn and focused on the next batter. His smile from the previous glory still prevailed.

"Where's Julie?"

"Sitting with that Mason boy," Andrew bobbed his head and rolled his eyes to the upper left bleacher. "I don't know why she's sitting with him, she's just sitting there with her earbuds in, thumbs clicking away on that iPhone...Go Bandits! We got this!"

Shelly took a look at her daughter, a small version of herself, lost in a world. She noticed the boy, who looked too nice to be with Julie. At least Mason saw the home run and was settling back in his seat next to their daughter.

"How did it go?" Andrew asked, not taking his eyes off the balls and strikes called by the black figure in the hot dust.

"The day was great, a really good showing," Shelly hesitated, confused by the immediate excitement that wasn't her own. She leaned in to his ear, "I think I sold my first house."

"Really?" Andrew asked, pausing his meditative, hopeful stare.

"Yes, really. Who did you think I am? A professional, of course," Shelly sat up and gave a cute smile at Andrew, then stole some of his popcorn. "And, I've got three more open houses every week for the next three weeks on the lesser properties represented by none other than Q…"

Crack. Andrew stood up, ignoring his wife for the moment while the Bandits crowd cheered again. The fifth batter in the lineup just hit a double which scampered past the Hornets' new pitcher. It hopped second base, and out to center field.

"Go! Go! Go! Hold up, hold up!" Andrew yelled, almost spilling his popcorn on his wife's lap as he jumped up with the rest of the parents.

Shelly just sat and looked confused. She never understood baseball, but she knew a home run was good. "Did we get another home run?" she asked as Andrew sat down.

"No dear, just a double. And there's two outs so Andy probably won't get up again this inning. What a game, huh?" Andrew said with a smile, then gave a small look of disappointment when he saw Shelly on her phone.

"What? Oh yes. It really is all very exciting." Shelly found a mistake on one of the online ads for her other property and was typing an email to correct the error. When she saw Andrew's face, she put away her phone.

The next batter up got caught looking at a third strike that barely made it on the outside corner of the plate. Andy's teammate, the runner on second, looked dejected as he walked back to get his hat and glove. The excitement subsided within the overrepresented Bandit crowd as people searched for hot dogs and more Coke.

"Who's buying it?" Andrew asked.

"What?" Shelly replied.

"The house, the Tudor, who's going to buy it?"

"Oh, you wouldn't believe! A nice couple from Winnipeg, a doctor and his wife. They just happened to see my ad and, he's Indian, or something."

"Or something? How did they know about the house?"

"The ad. The ad in the newspaper. They found it in a coffee shop while visiting. Didn't you see it on the fridge? I cut it out and put it there this morning."

"Oh yeah, yeah, I did. It was pretty nice. Will the deal go through you think?" Andrew's attention was beginning to refocus on the opposing team's first batter.

"It should, I've already been contacted. My first commission will pay for all of my promotional efforts so far and…"

Crack. Andrew stood again as the Hornets' opening batter rounded first base, but thought it better to stay put. The Bandits' right fielder grabbed a hopper and threw a scorcher to the second baseman which halted the runner.

Shelly became entranced as well. She watched their son between second and third base, pounding his glove every few seconds and squinting at the on-deck batter. As she watched him, he bit his lip and danced on his heels. She wondered if he had enough sunscreen. She was about to ask Andrew. As she turned to her husband, the words *enough sunscreen* fell away. He bit his lip and squinted too. She looked back at Andy and smiled, knowing that her husband probably looked the same thirty years ago on another ball field, far, far away.

Then, she cocked her head up at Julie and frowned. That Mason boy was trying to offer their daughter a hot dog but she refused. She kept incessantly tapping with her thumbs on her phone. Shelly wished she never got her that phone. She regretted requesting friendship to her daughter on Facebook. Julie had yet to respond to the friend request.

The next batter for the Hornets gave three empty swings and struck out. A larger boy came to the plate. The Bandit's coach gave a signal and the field players moved back a few feet.

"He's their heavy hitter, a Southpaw too," Andrew said with a confidential warning.

"What's a Southpaw?"

"A lefty."

"Oh, I see," Shelly said, back in the game. She was surprised at how serious everybody was at a kids' baseball game.

The boy did look menacing and a head taller than most of the other players. He took up position in the batter's box and clenched his teeth. Shelly saw that he had on what appeared to be *all the right gear*. His Nike cleats sparkled in the sunshine, his Oakley sunglasses reflected the glare. His gloved hands looked capable and brand new. She wondered if Andy had *all the right gear*. She would make sure that he did.

The large batter watched the first strike fly past, all the way to the catcher's mitt. He resettled his feet and awaited the next pitch.

Crack. He struck a hopper late and it sped fast toward Andy at shortstop. The boy reached for it as it came off its second bounce, caught it, and pivoted to make the quick throw to second. He did, and the second baseman threw a laser to first which called both runners out.

"A double play!" Andrew exclaimed. "Yes! I knew it, we practiced that pivot move and throw just yesterday." He beamed at Shelly in his excitement, and looked like he wanted to squeeze her, but didn't. "Do you want a hot dog?" he asked.

"Ah, sure." Shelly smiled at her husband. She saw Andy get more high fives and pats on the back as the

Bandits came in from the field.

Shelly scarfed down most of the hot dog, not realizing how ravenous she was. The next batters in the game were unknown to her, but she knew at some point, she would get to see Andy at bat.

"Oh, Hi Shelly. So good to see you," a woman said from above in the bleachers, coming closer.

Shelly turned and put her mostly eaten hotdog down next to Andrew and took up a napkin. "Hi Margaret, how are you?"

"Fine. Frank and I are fine. I saw your ad in the newspaper this morning. Well done. So quaint and special. Have any luck yet? How was the open house?"

"It was a good showing," Shelly said, wondering if she removed too much of her lipstick with the napkin.

"Good, glad to hear. I always knew you could make it out there. Holloway just isn't the same without you. Are you here to see your boy?"

"Yeah, and your son is on the, Hornets? Which one is he?" Shelly looked to the field.

"Oh, he's the relief pitcher out there now. He sure can throw a fast one."

Andy was preparing to be on deck. The bases had runners on first and second with two outs while the Bandits still maintained their comfortable lead. Andrew called his son over to the bleachers.

"Yeah Dad?" Andy looked ready for anything as he put on his helmet.

"This guy's throwing wild, so don't swing at any trash. Remember, a walk is as good as a single and will get you an RBI just the same."

"Got it Dad."

The women translated the interaction and turned back to their now, strangely affected conversation.

"Well, we better get back to the game. Good luck out there Shel. *Sell Sell Sell!*" Margaret said, using the old Holloway employee motto with a matching fake smile.

"Who was that?" Andrew asked as the first runner was walked.

"A snake," Shelly replied.

Andrew raised his brow and gave off a coy smile. "Andy is up next." He stood up, Shelly did the same in support of their son.

The first pitch was so fast and wild that the catcher lost it and had to scurry back to home, or risk giving up an easy run from a stolen base. The second pitch was wild too, but on the inside.

Andy did what his father told him, he kept his eye on the ball. He watched that unhittable ball past the mound, past the green, silver grass, all the way into his left thigh.

The pitch struck the boy so hard, the pain alone knocked the wind out of him as he slouched over with a quiet yelp. The umpire paused the game.

The couple rushed to their son as the coach helped the boy roll over. Andy was trying to hold back the tears but they gushed out anyway as he gave off that sad, baby face that Shelly remembered. She tried to hold him like she did all those long nights.

"I'm fine, I'm fine!" Andy yelled, waving his mom off.

"Oh, darling!" Shelly backed up and put her hands to her mouth as the men helped him up.

"We'll get a substitute runner, it's alright" the coach said.

"It's alright, son," Andrew repeated.

"But I want to play! We got them dad!"

"I know, I know, son. We'll get you home and have a look at that stinger there. Probably needs some ice."

Down at the lot, Shelly helped Andrew load their crying son into the Nissan. Realizing she was blocking her husband's exit, she got into her car to move, only to get out again.

"What about Julie?" she asked, tapping on her husband's window.

"Just park in my spot and go find her. She must have

seen what happened."

"Ok. We'll see you at home." She gave a look of concern to Andy laid out in the back seat, but he just looked away, wiping his tears.

When Shelly circled back around to park in her husband's spot, it was already taken. Three kids and a mom were piling out of a Camry, all with matching jerseys. She tried, but couldn't find another. Shelly dialed her daughter's phone, knowing that Julie had the thing six inches from her eyes.

No answer.

She texted their daughter and tried not to sound frantic.

She drove around the lot, and after a good while, found another coveted spot for her Mercedes. She marched her flats back to the game, but it was already over. Another set of teens had begun warming up. She searched around for Julie who was nowhere to be found. She didn't even see that Mason boy.

She texted and called again, only this time, a little more mean and demanding. After another hour of searching, she gave up.

No messages were returned.

Click! Click! Click! Click! Click! I couldn't get the

sound of Julie's texting out of my mind. Her phone may have made no sound, physically, but I could hear her fingers tapping against the glass. Click! Click! Click! I wasn't allowed to know what she was doing. She could have been blogging or writing an article. For all I knew, she could have been ordering an anti-mother device.

Andrew had Andy. The classic dad and son dynamic, but I didn't have anything with Julie. She wouldn't even let me call her by the name I gave her. I worked hard to create her tiny baby heart, and she wouldn't even give me the time of day. The way Julie treated me wasn't like a mommy.

A mommy is someone you ask for help. A mommy is someone that you look up to. No. No. Click! Click! Click! It was the sound of my forgotten ghost just trying to get to see her. I wanted my daughter to recognize me, to care about what I had to say. The more she touched the glass, the larger the walls became.

Even when I watched her click her thumbs on the phone that I gave her, I felt broken. It was like I gifted her a boat so we could sail the world together. Instead, she used it to sail as far away as she could be from all of us. Julie didn't even care about Andy's game. She didn't care that he hit a homerun and did a good job for his team. She didn't care that he got hit.

Click! Click! Click! She didn't care about anyone but herself. She didn't even care about Mason. My friends could see it, but that poor boy couldn't. He couldn't see that he was getting sucked into a glass prison. He was slowly getting trapped inside of her phone, and he didn't seem to care. He was such a nice, stupid boy. Bat of the eyelashes, a stray touch, and any man could be a pool of warm liquid.

I hoped deep down that she had lost her virginity to him. Just so he got something out of the deal. Before he was trapped inside of the glass like I was, waiting waiting waiting... for a pending notification. CLICK! CLICK! CLICK! She was always looking at her phone and she didn't see me call? She didn't see the red warning?

Honestly, I couldn't remember the last time that she said anything to me. Even when the game was over, and I waited around to make sure she wasn't dead in a ditch somewhere.

CHAPTER Four

It was taking her socks off, undressing into her bikini, and putting on her sandals that made Shelly calm down at least a little. The second wave came when Nina handed her a Daiquiri by the pool as the last shimmer of light in the day reflected off the clean water.

"Well, it sounds like you had a good day. You were a success," Nina stated, sipping her tropical wonder.

"I know, I know. It's just so hard to believe! I really hope the deal goes through. My first deal, can you imagine? Then, I can pay off what I borrowed for the initial marketing phase." Shelly sipped her drink, the cold alcohol washed down to her legs as she lay out in her wrapped bikini on the Chaise lounge next to Nina. Their sunglasses glinted and tickled each other's eyes.

"Borrowed? From Andrew? Why didn't he just *give*

you the money?" Nina asked.

"No, I took out a loan. I wanted to do Quintessential myself, at least at first."

"Oh, well, you should be fine then. Look at you, a businesswoman. At least Andrew is supportive. I can't get Gary to be interested in anything I want to try. Now that the kids are getting older, I have a lot of time during the week with that big empty house and this one." Nina petted their panting Golden Retriever, Frisk, who was finding his own respite in the shade under the lounge.

"Well, you could come work for me."

"Oh no, I couldn't pull it off, not the way you do. Besides, I like my weekends." Nina smirked at the Daiquiri, her third and yelled to her husband, "make sure mine is well-done, no bloody steaks for me!"

"Where's Julie?" Nina asked.

"I don't know, don't remind me."

"She'll be here in a few, bringing that Mason boy too," Andrew responded while flipping a burger, a cold bottle in his hand.

"How did you? Oh, never mind," Shelly sat back in defeat over losing the communication battle.

"Trouble with the teenage queen?" Nina asked with caution.

"I have no idea anymore," Shelly sighed into her

36

blended ice.

"So glad I had two boys. Before, they were a terror. Now, I let Gary handle the hard stuff, like punishment. I never thought I would say *wait 'till your father gets home,* but it does come in handy. Is that what's got you down? Is it Julie?"

"It's *Julia*, according to her anyway. I seemed to have just lost our connection. I tried to make a mommy-daughter date last week. She was less than thrilled about it. But, I had to cancel anyway to get my office leased on time. With Quintessential, everything is good, better than I hoped for. Everything is just as I dreamed. But it's like I'm almost waiting for the other shoe to drop. You should have seen the way that Margaret from Holloway was fishing for info. Shameless really."

"Well, that place was full of dirt bags anyway. Rich dirt bags, but they're all the same. It will all work out Shel, and I know you can do it. Can you rub some aloe on my shoulders?"

"Sure."

"Did you get her that present yet? Have you made any plans?"

"Yeah, I think so. Andrew bought her a Honda Fit last week, in a special teal blue, the one that she likes. Awful color, I think. We have a few weeks and I've already made reservations at the main clubhouse and with the caterer. I'm still looking for a DJ though."

"Well, let me know if you need help with the decorating. I don't have any sweet sixteen stuff on hand, but I could even order it for you if you get too busy. When is it again?" Nina leaned back to get a harder rub. What she seemed to really want was a massage by the pool.

"The twenty first. I should be able to wrap it up, but I'll let you know. I sent out the invitations after confirmation on the clubhouse. That was like pulling teeth, gosh. Getting her contact list from her and having her decide on who she actually wanted was near impossible."

"Yeah, she's got her little life in many different worlds. Do you think she is playing that Mason boy or what?" Nina asked.

"Yes. All she cares about right now is her future car and being editor in chief of that school paper. Mason is class president and a soccer stud. She probably gets leads out of him. And, he has a car."

"Have you read her articles? I think she is blogging now too. Seems she can write pretty good, for all I know." Nina sipped the last of her drink and placed her final cup down on the side for the dog to lick clean.

"I wouldn't know. I need to snatch a copy of that paper. It seems like her presence online is blocked for me, like a mommy firewall or something."

A black Dodge Charger pulled up to clubhouse

parking. Mason got out and opened Julia's door while holding her beach bag.

"Daddy, can you make me and Mason some burgers?"

"Sure honey. Hi Mason."

"Hello sir. Thanks for letting me swim."

"No problem. Cokes are in the cooler."

"Mason! Want to see my bruise?" Andy asked, running up to the tall teenager.

"Wow, that's a real stinger. I knew while he was warming up that Hornet relief pitcher threw trash. Hey, nice home run today kid."

"Thanks Mason!" recuperating Andy spun around and jumped in the pool.

"Julie, why didn't you answer me earlier? I looked all over for you," Shelly asked, setting down her drink.

Miffed, Julia took off her shorts and shirt to reveal a bikini as skimpy as her mom's. Also, Shelly noticed the shine of a violet and silver, unknown belly button ring. Julia turned her back, took Mason's hand, and they jumped in the pool. The cool water splashed onto Shelly's feet which left her in silence.

That night, with the kids tucked in bed with full bellies all around, Shelly stared at her husband as he slept. Still in his swim trunks, his body was only half covered and his tanned skin shined past his dark chest hair. She wanted to grope him, make him get a rise in reaction, but she stopped short.

His smart jaw and Saturday stubble formed a smile below his easy hair. Shelly didn't know what he was thinking to cause him to smile as he slept, probably baseball. She didn't want to break into his happy thoughts. Instead, she curled up next to him. She could smell the faintness of beer still on his breath, mixed with barbeque and sunshine. She wanted to caress his face, but did so only in her mind, as she felt herself fall into a peaceful sleep.

She showed up dressed like that, dressed like me.

Click! Click! Click! She probably got the belly button ring to spite me for canceling on her. She was going to do it no matter what. I would give up the time that she didn't even want from me. I wanted to make a scene. I wanted to scream and tell her that she couldn't have a birthday anymore.

Until she cared about my feelings, the woman who birthed her, then she was to receive no birthday. I kept my lips held shut, because no matter how cold the glass of my prison got, I still wanted to see her, even in passing. Click! Click! Click! I wasn't going to cancel her party, I couldn't. What I wished was that she would treat me less like a snide mother and more like mom. The kind of mom that would have taken her to get the belly button ring. Just put up a bit of a fight.

Click! Click! Click! And Andrew. Talking down to me like I don't understand anything. Southpaw? Southpaw? Isn't it literally just as easy to say lefty? What do paws have to do with baseball? Is there even a Northpaw?

He didn't even care to hear how my sale went today. And why? Because our son loves him and he loves our son, which is dandy. Apparently, our daughter loves him too. Everything has always been her fault. She ruined our lives. Everyone loved Andrew. Then, Julia came along.

Click! Click! Click! Everyone in that entire parking lot didn't know how to park. It was like they all came in pregaming, drinking liquor by the fistfuls. Turns out that the lines are a suggestion instead of actual boundaries. I wasn't invited to the meeting where they voted on that.

I feel as though, I'm not invited to anything. I feel unwanted. Even Andrew seems uncaring. He would rather pay attention to something as mundane as baseball than hear about my day. It is just a stick and a ball. A stick and a ball.

Click! Click! Click! I could still see her fingernails against the glass. My message lighting up to tell her that her brother was hurt. Click! Click! Click! Her perfect witchlike fingernails scraping across the screen that I gave her. Another message and another phone call. There was no way that she couldn't see that I was worried or that I was trying to contact her. Click! Click! Click!

She left me in the dark. In the cold. My mind cycled around ideas to get back at her. The harsh rays of the sun bounced off the desert concrete. Click! Click! Click!

She was not about to take away my happiness. Click! Click! Click! Couldn't people see that I had things I cared about? I read every one of Julie's articles. They never showed the slightest interest in what I was doing. I wondered what would happen if I stayed home instead of going to work, not making dinner, sitting in the dark, unmoving. Would they notice?

No. No. They wouldn't notice. They'd walk by me like I was some sort of statue. Click! Click! Click! The glass in the phone replacing my solemn expression. They wouldn't even notice if I died.

As my hand was placed against Andrew's chest, I could smell the alcohol on his breath. I felt how warm he was against my ice cold, statue skin. Click! Click! Click! Click! Click! Click! Click! As I concentrated on the clicking of her Phoenix, and the messages she was sending to everyone around me, I could feel Andrew's skin become cold against mine again.

He was dead to the world before I could even tell him how the open house went. I was so angry at him, but I didn't want to wake him. Click! Click! Click! The tapping. It wouldn't stop. It sounded like nails on a chalkboard or a needle scratching glass. Click! Click! Click! Even though my anger was all encompassing, sleep was starting to creep through my arms and legs. In a moment, I was going to be lost in a world of dreams, but tomorrow, I was going to bask in the glory of my successful business.

MARC D. CREPEAUX & A.M. HOUNCHELL

CHAPTER Five

"Why don't you just stick around awhile? We'll sleep in, I'll make breakfast. We'll send the kids off somewhere, we'll sleep in again," Andrew said, groping like a boy from his fixed position on the bed.

"We already slept in, at least a little. Besides, you had your chance last night, funny man. Instead, you knocked right out." Shelly was putting in her earrings and was already half dressed in front of her large vanity. She sat and spoke to her reaching husband through the mirror and smiled with a slight blush at his own immaturity.

"I know, I was so tired," Andrew yawned. "Must have been all that sun."

"Must have been the beer and steaks," Shelly giggled. "I have had two phone calls already to show

Porter Lane this morning. I expect I'll have a few more, maybe on the tudor even. I won't be long though, probably back by three. Have any plans?"

"Clean the garage," Andrew said, defeated in his Sunday morning sexual conquest. "We'll probably take a dip and, who knows?" Andrew slid both his arms behind his head with his elbows cocked. He showed off his bare chest and bulging swim trunks in one last effort at seduction.

"Make sure Andy wears sunscreen," Shelly said as she added fake blush to her already fading cheeks. "Do you know what Julie has planned? Maybe she'll want to go with me?"

"I doubt it, she won't wake up for another hour or two. Any idea when Mason brought her home? I meant to stay up to administer curfew punishment but I…"

"Curfew punishment?" Shelly giggled at the thought. "And how do you suppose you were going to do that? No, she only came home fifteen minutes late. I tried to tell her goodnight but all I got out of her was a groan and a run up the stairs."

"She's going through a weird time. I can't explain it," Andrew rolled over in defense.

"Well, I certainly don't expect *you* to, but I can. I just wish she would open up to me more. I wish I could *get through*. How do you get through to her? She answers your texts and calls. Some kind of special app?" Shelly plopped on the bed next to Andrew, fully made-up and smiled.

"No," Andrew groped at the distraction in front of him. Shelly's blouse wasn't all the way buttoned and he lost his words to the battle once again.

"Well, you seem to know how to talk to her," Shelly caught his hand.

"I'm just genuinely interested in what she is doing. What she is writing, where she is going, who she's with."

"And I'm not?"

"Sure you are, but I find an angle. My angle is goofy Dad angle, harmless really. She responds to that. I make her explain things like Instagram or Snapchat, even though the twenty years olds at work are all about it. Even though I design software and have already read about it in my monthlies. I've been correcting her writing for as long as she could write, and she still asks me to do that at least."

"But that's the point, Andrew, she asks you to. She doesn't ask anything from me but money. Money, when she probably already got some from you. What about punishments? What about the hard stuff? For me, it seems like it's all the hard stuff."

"Well, I'm not overbearing…" Andrew looked away at his word.

"And I am? *Listen to that*. Why do I have to be the

bad guy?"

"I was saying, I'm not overbearing, but I'm not a pushover either. She knows I draw the line in the sand and she doesn't cross. Sure, she tiptoes around the line."

"Tiptoes, huh?" Shelly gave a girlish smirk at her husband as he laid back with his silly notions of justice.

"I'm also available. Anytime, anywhere, I'm there for her. Listen, I know you are just starting this thing out, but the idea was to put in hard work now, so you don't have to down the road. Eventually, you will need some employees. That way, you won't have to be gone most weekends, leaving us to our own devices."

"I know, but it's what I have to do." Shelly stopped short and the question *Why?* rolled over her mind. This was brushed away as she fluffed her hair.

"I can't believe she is going to be sixteen soon, gosh," Andrew said into the bed. "Did you call the DJ yet? Do you want me to?"

"No, I'll do it on my way back. Today. Did you check on the car, I mean, really check?"

"Yeah, but what's to check? It's new. It's her color, she picked it out, basically. I just paid and set it all up. It'll be here in time and I'll get the big bow. Geez, my parents never got me a new car for my sixteenth, not even for Clair or Monica."

"Well, your parents weren't as well off, and your

sisters, don't get me wrong, not as bright."

"Yeah, I know. The things we do for love…"

Andrew grabbed and dipped Shelly on the bed for one last advance. She allowed it, even for the moment, and kissed Andrew with passion and romantic tease. He tried for a third advance but she stopped his hand.

"I know Andrew, but I'll be back later. Then, who knows?" Shelly grabbed him hard, momentarily paralyzing her husband before slipping away to the bathroom to doll up the final touches.

"Well, you could at least ask her. Who knows? Invite her to lunch?" Andrew yelled into the direction of the bathroom.

"You're right! I'll go check in on her once I'm done."

Shelly tiptoed across the long hall and silent carpet to the other side of the house. She tapped lightly on Julie's door, no answer. She knocked louder, "Julie?"

The door opened with the last rap which revealed a colorful and fairly messy suite. A spaghetti strap lay on the floor in front of the door and Shelly instinctively picked it up and started to fold it until she heard the sound of the shower and let it go.

The steam came from Julie's bathroom as a child trapped inside a young woman's body sang through the mist. Shelly stopped short and didn't say a word, just stood outside the door and listened to the beautiful voice as she showered.

That was her voice, her own child trapped inside. Shelly danced back into the memory of baths and bubbles, mixed with old vinyl, and her mother. From her own childhood, she remembered her now dead mother and her tears. Then, dripping the salts of joy from childbirth, her own child, Julie.

Julie, who ran into puddles while she giggled past missing teeth and boyish hair. Julie, who sat on her lap when Shelly read her stories in a bright voice. All those years ago when she stayed and kept a home. The little girl burned into her memory, those eyes looking up at her through tears when the hurt came. Those wispy moments of laughter when she tried to teach Julie how to bake cookies for the bake sale. Julie looked up to her then, she thought Shelly was a hero of the kitchen and home.

Where did it go wrong? Was it after her first period? Could it be that simple? How much time would they last without a connection? When will it end? When will her little girl ask her to play again?

"Eww! Get out!" Julie slammed the bathroom door on her mother and fired the blow dryer in a second shot across the bow.

Shelly stumbled back, startled. She became angry and made to bang on the door. Instead, she held the invisible baby in her arms again and looked around at the large and foreign, teenage room.

She left without saying a word and drove on without radio or tear.

Andrew acted like I didn't want to sleep in later, but I did. I wanted to act like my daughter almost every morning. I had a drive that wouldn't let me stay in bed. It ripped me from my bed and forced me to put my makeup on.

It sang like a morning bird, letting me know exactly how to place my makeup. It even fought Andrew's advances for me. It was more than I was, like my auto-pilot. I caught my face in the mirror out of vanity.

I looked like a ghost. My face was void of color, giving me the shade of death. I applied some blush, trying to force color. I pressed it to my face like clay, trying to look fuller and human, but it looked more like I had a bad paint job.

I almost didn't recognize myself in the mirror, but that had been happening for so long. I remembered being so young, but I was getting strands of grey hair and dark spots under my eyes. Why did I look so old? When did I get this old? My eyes were dull and grey, and I didn't remember what color they were supposed to be.

Click! Click! Click! I heard the tapping of fingers on glass. My image was tapping back at me, trying to tease me in my old age. I turned away from the mirror and took up talking to Andrew.

He tried to explain in elegant phrases and long-winded discussion that he wasn't as hard on our daughter. He tried to accuse me of being a hard ass, and I was unsure how to take it. I felt like I was the bad guy. Andrew and Julie both treated me like I was secondary. She liked him more. It was clear.

Click! Click! Click! The sound of my daughter tapping the glass cage of a wild animal. Yet, she viewed me as a fish in a bowl, swimming around, easy to manipulate. She only ever needed me for money and she could squeeze.

I tiptoed along the edge of the carpet, feeling like a tiger trying to catch a gazelle off guard. The end tables in the hall and the door to her bedroom were my tall grass. Another step, another step.

Her room was like an alien world. Slathered in purples and pinks and bright colors.

I heard Julie singing. I moved towards the door, attracted by her voice. I wanted to click too. I wanted to sing with her.

She didn't love me. I remembered holding her, thinking how beautiful she was in my arms. Now, there was a rift between us, so large it altered my memories. One moment she was in my arms, a baby, helpless, and waiting for me. Then, in another moment, I was holding nothing. I had nothing. She was a ghost.

Then, as I thought about it even more, I realized that I was a ghost. I looked back at my arms, trying to summon the vision of a baby again, but it wouldn't happen. I needed her to need me. If she didn't need me, what did it really matter how hard I worked? My flesh and blood didn't care. Her betrayal was internal, like if my heart decided to commit suicide. She was my suicidal heart.

I kept trying to feel the baby in my arms, but she wouldn't reappear. I was standing in a foggy abyss, staring at arms in the darkness and red flowed.

Julie was in the doorway, staring like I was a tiger.

Her screams produced a fire that pushed me away further than I'd been before. I ran from her domain filled with foreign articles and colors. I looked at my arms again, but they were empty. My heart wasn't there.

MARC D. CREPEAUX & A.M. HOUNCHELL

CHAPTER Six

"So, what you're saying," Shelly glanced at her husband who sat in his own uncomfortable chair, and swallowed hard. "You're saying that our daughter is a *bully*?"

"In a way, yes. Julia seems to think that she can crush others by defaming them. It is clear to me what she wants is to be editor in chief of the newspaper. Usually, kids are bullied for weird hair or poor choice in clothing. But in this case, your daughter seems to be all about *the power play*."

Loretta Daniels, the principle of Treemont High, pushed back her long, brown hair behind her bifocals. Her dark skin matched her mahogany desk and her eyes looked thoughtfully at the concerned couple sitting in hard, wooden chairs before her. She referenced a note amid a stack of papers on her desk and slid off her candy red glasses which were attached to a gold chain around her neck. Principal Daniels then handed the note to Shelly.

"*Reorder yourself or face the consequences*?" Shelly read and looked at her husband. During school functions and the like, Andrew spoke less and Shelly often took the lead when talking to other parents and teachers they didn't already have an acquaintance with. This meeting was no different as Andrew barely spoke and let Shelly ask all the questions.

"*Reorder yourself?* That hardly sounds threatening. I mean, what are we talking about, really?"

"Well, Candice Montgomery, the editor in chief now, is a senior and was running for class vice-president. I know that Mason Laurant, the current President and your daughter *go together*, and there is some jealousy which is apparent. Five underclassmen were recently caught on camera, taking all Candice's posters down, but leaving some of them up, ah, with *terrible* alterations. I am still trying to get to the bottom of this. I know they were put up to it, but none of them talked until I mentioned the word *expulsion*. Then, they sang like little birds. It seems your Julia paid them to conduct vandalism."

At that, Andrew let out a worried sigh and the note seemed to melt in Shelly's hands. Before it could, she set it on the desk and listened in horror for more.

"She messed with the layout last night, and the first run of the paper came out with a blazing article, an editorial, written by Candice Montgomery, on why she shouldn't have any position in student government, why she should resign the paper."

Principal Daniels handed the morning edition to the couple who read it together.

She continued as they read, "Of course, this has been taken out and corrected but it seems to me that Julia thinks that she does everything for the paper and should get every reward. I can assure you that Candice is a fine student and has worked just as hard. She is a senior now and this is the usual progression of things. For her status, I mean."

Shelly let what the principal was saying trail off in her mind as she took in the editorial. By the third paragraph, Julia had her mother tied up in a web and she commented to herself on how good the writing really was. She stopped from saying so out loud and handed the rest to Andrew so he could finish.

"Now, we are willing to let this slide, in a way, and chalk it all up to misdirected ambition. If Julia will agree to an admission of her guilt in these situations, apologize to Candice, and serve after-school suspension for the rest of the year, we won't have anything else to say about this subject." Principle Daniels put her bifocals back into their position from around her neck and began to shuffle some papers on her desk.

Before the parents could answer, Shelly noticed how perfect the principal's nails were. They had a high gloss, and were painted a somber pink that clashed with her candy red glasses. Despite the spring, the woman had some depth to her wardrobe which seemed to accent her dark skin. She imagined the world that this woman lived, she was likely an educator most of her adult life. Shelly rode with her in her Mercedes, in her mind, every day, and every day with the kids and their problems and her coffee and the soft leather case that was propped behind her desk. She wondered what Mr. Daniels was like, probably an educator himself, or was this *her thing*?

Loretta Daniels coughed between paper shuffling and waited for a response. A thing she had likely done thousands of time to students and parents alike over the many years behind a teacher's desk.

Andrew stayed glued to the newspaper and gave a terrified look as Shelly turned to him. He was outgoing with a charismatic personality, once you got to know him. But here, in this setting, Shelly thought he acted like *he* committed these crimes and was paying the price sitting in that uncomfortable chair. Like he was a little boy in trouble. Andrew was of no use right now, in defense of their daughter, or otherwise. Shelly again took the lead.

"But if she has after school suspension, she won't be able to work on the paper anymore. What about her writing? I know it is important to her," Shelly mustered the first of the negotiations on behalf of the parents on trial."

"Precisely." Principle Daniels smacked down a paper on her desk with the word and Andrew almost jumped out of his chair. "You will need to monitor her social media as well. I am getting some reports from parents who care that Julia is launching another front there. Please see this as a warning that I hope she will take seriously. Julia is not to post anything about this or Candice on her social media. If I hear about it, there will be consequences. I believe that it is in the best interest of your child to take a time out from that which both gives her the greatest joy and the most hardship. She is trying to do too much in this case, and it would be better than getting kicked out of the newspaper team for the rest of her time here at Treemont. I recognize that your daughter is a good student and that she cares, but, if we do not nip this idea she has about becoming the queen of the newspaper early, she will get herself into more trouble than she is already in. Let me remind you that I have every right to call for her to be expelled with these games. I will not as long as she complies with what we think is best."

"Oh, I see. *Expelled*?" Andrew finally chimed in and gave a serious look for what Shelly thought was the effect.

"Yes. Expelled. And it is up to you to convince her that by admitting her guilt, apologizing, and taking a break from the paper…that these deeds are in her best interest."

"Yes ma'am, we'll do just that, no problem," Andrew spoke again for the both of them from his humble corner.

Shelly wanted to fight more in there, even turned to Andrew as they walked back to their separately parked cars. Back into the adult Tuesday afternoon, back from their emergency break from their respective jobs. Instead, Andrew marched with purpose to his SUV, ignoring his wife.

He turned just before getting in like a gunslinger at the final moment in a duel and said, "I'll handle it Shel, don't worry."

"OK Andrew." Shelly stood there and watched as he drove away. The sound of quick tires met pavement and gravel which filled her ears as she paused at the scene around her with the driver side door open.

Children played flag football, while some chased a Frisbee behind a high, metal fence. A fence that even the breeze seemed to get through.

If you spend enough time with a desk, eventually you become a desk.

While she talked and I stared at the desk I wanted to

strangle her. Or bash her head in. She wanted to destroy my daughter's life for nothing. She barely did anything.

When I read her article, I could see how great her writing was. But even with Andrew's help, she was still making casual errors. It didn't matter, other than the fact that I could have helped her. I could have helped her instead of Andrew, but she didn't care about me.

Then it struck me as the desk continued talking at us. She was going to take the one thing that Julie cared about away from her. My teeth and claws prepared to strike her.

Andrew decided to grow a spine. He tried for sex harder than he tried to help our daughter. Our own flesh and blood. My teeth and claws turned towards Andrew, but he still wasn't paying attention. If I could have just defended, then it could have restored her love in me.

How hard would it be for a lion to kill a desk? I wasn't about to find out, because Andrew's spine held me like a rope. Click! Click! Click! I heard the tapping on the glass, but it sounded weaker and weaker. Click! I felt Julie's strength weakening as my heart picked up pace. My blood pulsed, but I couldn't justify striking.

When my anger faded, Andrew was telling me that he would handle it, but I didn't think he would. Julie was going to be as pissed off as she had ever been, and I knew that anger. She got it from my side of the family. It would be easier for me to talk to her. I wanted to, but it wasn't *a good idea.*

I looked back at the school, maybe I could still go back now that Andrew was gone from me. It wasn't the worst idea I'd ever had. Before I made my decision, I watched the children playing. Each of them had a mother who loved them. They each had a mother who would die for them. I wasn't going to die fighting the incarnation of a desk. I had a decision to make, but I knew the repercussions of both choices.

If I ran into the school to confront Principle Desk, then I could make everything worse for Julie. The positive side of that was that I could threaten someone.

The alternative was to give up, and it would definitely loosen the last few ropes which tied my life to Julie's. She would never blame Andrew. She would blame me, because I was there. She'd lose her job, run off with some boy to South Dakota, and she'd only come back to ditch a mistake, on me.

Click.

The last click was weak. It sounded like the screeching of a rusted keyboard. I wanted to help. I wanted to make it all go away.

CHAPTER Seven

Traffic was lethargic as Shelly weaved through the muck to her new office. The cars didn't jam up at lights as they usually did. People seemed to hesitate while pushing go at intersections and craned at unhurried workers. Shelly occasionally used her horn to call out a few who were in the collective trance. The overcast haze and laziness of the drones could only mean doom.

As she went to open her office door, there was a flyer for Chinese food. Shelly remembered that she didn't eat breakfast. She frowned at the unappetizing color photos but stuffed the menu in her purse anyway for future late nights in her new home.

As she turned the hard key and took in the stale air, Shelly frowned. She remembered the shipment of furniture did not come through yet. She also wished that she brought a soapy sponge and paint brush instead of her laptop. Everything was happening out of order, and because she was the sole proprietor, this meant she was at fault.

No need to meet clients here yet anyway, only perhaps to close a deal. Even then, she might go where they were, especially if her furniture wasn't there yet. Her only deal so far was for the Tudor and the couple coming from someplace in Canada. Everything would be accomplished using drop boxes and innocent emails.

Shelly cracked open her laptop and sat carefully at the bare desk which was left by the last tenant. She looked around in disgust and thought about calling a cleaning service, and a painter. The leasing office said the place would be ready by now, perhaps they forgot to spruce up the off-white. Perhaps they forgot about her altogether. She pushed that thought aside. If she had to do it herself, she would get dirty and paint on one of those long nights. Furniture or no furniture, Andrew or no Andrew.

The glimmer on the nice picture window speckled for a moment and Shelly thought again about Julie- she should have invited her daughter to celebrate the occasion. They could have ordered Chinese, could have had a heart to heart about the trouble at the school. But at this rate, Shelly wouldn't likely be back for dinner. Besides, Andrew said he would take care of it. Shelly spent so much time getting money-makers ready that she often neglected her own refuge.

Outside, in the mini-mall parking lot, Shelly noticed a college couple with car trouble standing on the hot blacktop. The girl had a bikini top and torn jean shorts that hinted at her trouble, and a belly ring that sparkled for everyone. Shelly thought of Julie, and if the two free-spirited girls went to the same sleazy shop. The college tramp pranced her slender, tanned body around in flip-flops, her bleach-blonde hair up, and giggled at her boyfriend. He opened the hood and scratched his scruffy head in confusion as Shelly stood up in the window to watch.

The girl leaned up against the lime-green Mustang with teal racing stripes and lit a cigarette. Shelly watched as the coed smoked with the intent of pleasuring every male driver who turned their neck to watch. The rear bumper was rusting off. Shelly let thoughts seep in about the couple and that rotting bumper. They didn't belong here in this neighborhood, this reality. Drug runners in a precarious position, most likely.

As her laptop hummed alive, Shelly was distracted from the couple by a buzz on her phone from the electronic gods in the sky. She recognized without opening that it was a message from the buyers of the Tudor. She waited to open the email on her computer, where she could do more damage. Where she could click and clack with ease, using all her fingers, maximizing the potential of distant communication.

She waited for the page to load on the computer and glazed over the words with her rapid eyes. She recognized the phrasing, the verbs, and the tone. The deal was over. It was all a dream. A dream, minced down through an electronic sausage gauntlet and spat out in front of her on the bare desk, all over her keys, all over her hands. They weren't buying the house after all. They found a better deal. They took a few more vacation days and found another, better house. They looked around more, without her. They evaded her presence.

She thought about sending something polite back, or something nasty. Perhaps a sweet and innocent message with a little tinge on the end, like she knew how, like she taught Julie. She thought about straight politeness but it wasn't called for, not this time. Her fingers hovered over the keyboard, still with the splattered gore, and she wrote nothing.

Instead, she shut her laptop and bit her lower lip. She cried, staring out at the couple and their innocence. Their vague recollection of sanity. Their freedom.

Bars trapped her, and bars would keep her safe. These dusty, white walls, these windows. They were all for safety. The safety of time. They held her in, made her make plans, made her miss time with the family. These undecorated walls, this filthy pedestal. No one knew their charm, not like Shelly.

How much the walls of this safe interior could give, and how much they could take away. No one knew just how problematic her life had become. No pills or undying devotion could seem to render. It was all inappropriate.

She wanted then to murder the couple outside, but it was inappropriate. It wasn't right for her to march out there, mid-morning with her heels, scoop one off and jab it into the giggling tramp's eye. Just because they were free. What did that say about her? Would that seal her fate too?

What if she just told them to go away? Away from her window. She didn't want to be bothered by freedom outside. She didn't want to see anything but bars. She could cover the window, but somehow that wouldn't make them go away.

She could help them, yes. She could help them, call them a cab or drive them somewhere herself, drugs and all, who cares. At least they would be gone. Away from her misery, away from her failure. Away from her comfortable prison.

After all my failures. White walls were comforting like glossy tile or clean sheets. It was perfect. I wanted to tell everyone about their potential. I wanted to color the walls with bright blood reds. I wanted the walls to speak to me. If I sat at my keyboard long enough, they'd tell me it's okay.

The thing about walls is, they never move. Walls listen and keep me safe. Not like the couple, who jetted away from me without considering my feelings. They should have known I had feelings. Everyone has feelings except them.

I slammed shut, and I could hear the walls laughing at me. My pain reverberating through my feet. As I approached a window, I saw two teens standing by a car. They were a threat to the sanctuary I'd created. If they came closer, they'd bleed the happiness they'd lied to themselves about through the walls. I didn't need that.

The walls were comfort. Separate them all from my kingdom. They'd have to ask permission to come and bring me food. I'd sit cross-legged on my desk, waiting for them to tell me what hellish nightmare was going on outside. I'd be safe, quintessentially safe. That was my reality.

I would wait on my desk, safe from the outside world until someone cared enough to come see me, but they never would. My spineless husband would forget, my daughter would never look up from her phone, and they'd all starve me out.

I'd stay safe, and laugh at their misgivings. They thought that they could do so well without me, but they didn't know what it was like to be alone. They didn't know what I was going through. The walls kept laughing, soaking in the tasteless happiness outside.

Salt makes everything better. It does when mixed with iron. That's why sadness is so important, because sadness brings the salt of tears. Happiness is nothing in comparison. I wanted everyone who'd ever been happy to die a horrible death, while I stayed safe in my hopes and dreams.

Why was everyone betting against me? I didn't need to ask myself that, because I knew why people bet against things. Everyone was under the assumption that I would fail. Oh, but they were in for a surprise. My kingdom was going to rise from the ashes.

I crawled under my desk to escape the sounds of laughter and giggling. Half-naked slut, trying to take advantage of some dumb teenage boy pumped with hormones. Well, she wasn't going to take advantage of my solitude. She wasn't going to get her tentacle grip into my fortress. I was safe. When they left, that's when I'd leave. If they never left, I'd just stay under the desk. No whore could take what I'd created away from me. None of them could. If she tried, I'd kill her. I would. She shouldn't test me.

I clutched my pen, staring at the perfectly white wall. Except it wasn't perfect. I moved closer until my nose was touching the hot paint. There was a black speck on my perfect white wall. A single stain, thinking it could get by me. I yanked the scissors from my desk and scratched the paint away from the walls. It would all be perfect again, and everyone would continue to love me. I scratched and scratched, trying to clear the wall of its horrible blemish, caused by the tainted happiness outside.

CHAPTER Eight

Shelly rubbed the suntan lotion over her long legs as she watched the younger version of herself do the same. Julia did so without conversation and her mother couldn't see the rolling thoughts behind the teenager's dark sunglasses.

Andrew was the only one of the pair to have talked to the girl who had been grounded without electronics after her near expulsion. The mother-daughter combo had done quite a bit of sun tanning and swimming together the summer before, but had not yet begun the tradition this year. The events leading up to this summer created a stale relationship. Shelly hoped to fix that, despite the bad timing of the opening of Quintessential Realty and her own failures in that effort.

"You going for a swim?" She asked with a kind

smirk.

Julia looked over the water and scrunched her face like her father, tilted her glasses up, and somehow gauged the temperature of the pool with her squint.

"Ah, not quite yet," Julia determined, "I want to get sunned a little first. Are you?"

"I was thinking the same thing, get a little warmed before any big splash." Shelly smiled, but did not receive the same back, only a nod as Julia moved her towel to lay down.

Julia immediately tried to click away at her phone, shading the screen with one hand. When this didn't work, she gave up and set it under the towel. The girl paused at the waves and the shimmering light. She held her breath, about to say something, then stopped.

Shelly tried to not stare at her in expectation for the big talk. It was then that the same visions of her little girl came back into focus. Yes, she was turning into a young woman, and arguably prettier than her mother. Yet, there was still this youthful groan about her, like a hungry baby hoping to make the right sounds to get attention. Shelly felt then like a gentle giant. She wanted to scoop up the baby and coo the small creature back to sleep. She wanted to tell her daughter that despite the tough circumstances, everything was going to be alright.

"Did you call and hire the DJ yet?" Julia asked, breaking the trance.

"Yes, everything's set." Shelly responded in a panic. She forgot to hire the DJ, hadn't done anything to help with the party since the fallout of the Tudor sale. She had only stuck her head in work sand. She busied herself the only way she knew how- showing houses like a mad woman and contacting new leads.

"And you got my song list?"

"Yes, I sent it along," Shelly lied about that too. She had peered at the song list, and with nothing recognizable except for a few of the top forty she had heard on the radio, Shelly let it drown in her email inbox with hundreds of other messages.

Things had calmed down a little after the meeting with the principle and Andrew's talk with Julia. The grounded teenager spent several days unwilling to come out of her room. Just today, she received her phone back after a whole week without it. The previously unattached appendage had been set on the kitchen counter, fully charged and in a new case, courtesy of Andrew.

When Shelly first saw it there in the kitchen, she wanted to throw it out the window or grind it up with the garbage disposal. She thought that it would distract the withdrawing teen from their swim together. Instead, Julia tapped here and there during Special K, giggled a few times, and set it down to concentrate on the soggy flakes.

Andrew must have done a decent job of informing their daughter of her punishment, both in school and at home. He always had a way with presenting the gravity of the situation at hand. Shelly wasn't home, but it must have been heartbreaking and dramatic for Andrew to tell her what she had to do to make things right.

According to Andrew, who was of course light on the details, Julia went into a rage at first, but eventually calmed down and agreed to apologize. All thanks to Andrew, she took it on the chin and would eventually come around.

Shelly wanted to broach the subject but wasn't sure how at first. "Do you want to read *Cosmo*?" That was all she could ask while holding up the magazine, an offering. They used to do that all the time, compare notes on fashion trends, makeup, and sometimes giggle about boys.

"No *Mom*, you go ahead, I'm ok," she said with a raised palm.

"Why not dear?"

"Because…because it is bad writing *Mom*, and I don't want to read bad writing."

"Oh, I see. But, you used to like it."

"That was before I knew it was bad Mom. Just, never mind. You go on ahead."

Shelly felt the emphasis of disdain on the word, her title, *Mom*. She wondered where her daughter had learned to jab so, and hoped it wasn't from her own mouth. She flipped through some of the pages of the gaudy magazine. She tried to read but couldn't ingest or seem to figure what was bad about the writing. She felt self-conscious, small for enjoying the supposed trash all these years, for listening to the advice.

Perhaps Julia was right, it was all garbage, made to look perfect with glossy photographs and airbrush. Then, she knew just how to broach the subject that lingered on her mind.

"We are proud of you," Shelly said, closing the magazine.

"What?"

"Your father and I, we are proud of you, all that you've accomplished- the paper, your writing, your grades."

"I don't understand," the teenager sat up like she was about to run to the movies with her friends.

"That doesn't mean you aren't grounded or suspended. I do think you need some help with directing your, uh, energy and efforts. Also, your treatment of people could use a little work. What we are proud of is your ambition, and your intellect. I read your article that had to get cut from the paper, it was great, *mean*, but great. I know that I may not know what great writing is, but I do think you will find your way, learn from your own battles. Who knows? Maybe you will be a published author someday." Shelly grew a warm smile on her face and took off her sunglasses at the teenager.

"Um…thanks, I guess?" Julia squirmed a little as she felt the doting of her mother's attention but would not smile back. She broke the interaction by yawning and standing up as she stretched. Shelly watched as the petite version of herself in a bikini ran down the diving board and splashed into the waiting oasis.

Mother followed daughter. All were cleansed.

The tapping was finally gone, and scratching had faded when I was sitting next to the pool. The water was so on my mind. She was almost a carbon copy of me like God had just pressed copy and paste on his magic keyboard. She had my younger body, but she was the same, except she acted different.

She treated me like I knew nothing. I wanted to love her, but I wished she was still a baby. I needed her to be a toddler again, so she could waddle around the pool and need me to save her from drowning. I needed her to drown.

It was clear that she preferred her father, based on how much she spoke to him, even though I was the one who sacrificed everything for them. I didn't eat, I hardly slept, and I stayed locked in my perfect white room.

No. No. No. They treated me like a lab rat. Like a dumb lab rat looking for cheese. Julie didn't even think I could read well enough to know what wasn't good writing. She thought I was an idiot, but she had much more in common with the whore out the window. She didn't want to speak to me. Julie wanted to poison with oversaturated fat through the glass.

Click! Click! Click! I needed that glass between us, or she could get into my fortress. She would be able to smudge the perfect walls. If that happened, I'd need thirty pairs of scissors to peel her grimy fingerprints off the wall.

The joke was on her. I knew what good writing was, because I was a realtor with my own job. I had my own ad below the weather. It was a perfect sunny day above my ad, and that's how it was going to stay.

I'd coil my arm around her perfectly tanned neck, and I would keep her out of harm's way. Eventually, she had to thank me. For now, I had to let her keep her perfectly fabricated happiness, so she didn't feel smothered. Before I locked her in my fortress, she needed to have the best sweet sixteen. I was going to have to make everything perfect. After that, I'd sneak up on her and keep her in my clutches like the lioness I was.

She didn't know it, but she was already drowning, and I was going to save her. I knew the party was my last chance to keep her. If the party didn't work for her, then I would find myself on opposite sides of the glass from her and everyone forever. She was the only success that I wanted in my fortress of white walls. Julie was the one *who suggested Quintessential Realty as the name, and I just wanted to live up to her expectations.*

Click! Click! Click! She was my only success. No matter how much I tried, I couldn't sabotage her. I'd throw anyone under the bus to save her.

In a startled panic, I stood up, with glossy eyes. I didn't remember where her list of music was. Where did I put it?

Click! Click! Click! That wasn't coming from the glass between us. That clicking was in my chest. My lungs couldn't fill my chest with air, and I started to panic. I fell to one knee. I was never going to find the list. And that was going to be the end of it.

Julie would drown, and I would be helpless, trapped even.

CHAPTER nine

"Welcome, welcome! I'm so glad you could make it," Shelly said, opening the heavy door with ornamental trim and a speckled window for the young couple. Shelly tried not to frown at them as she peered at their aging Honda Civic in the driveway. It still had the college stickers and she wondered if they were at the wrong open house. She wanted to hide her own face.

"Oh wow, it's even better than in the pictures," the young woman cooed into the open foyer.

Focusing on the task, Shelly shook both of their hands, and said with a commercial rhythm, "I'm Shelly with Quintessential Realty."

"I'm Lance and this is my girlfriend Annette." The young man was casual with no ring on his finger. He pointed to the dining area in the next room, "Oh, look at that wainscoting honey, isn't that classic?"

"And, will this be your first home?" she guessed with an eye of disdain.

"Yep. We rent right now but are looking for a better neighborhood. Plus, we got one on the way," Lance patted his girlfriend's belly. They groped each other right in front of her and giggled.

Perky and blonde Annette didn't show at all and Shelly wondered if this was a trick. This open house on Cambridge Lane was already without guests an hour into the showing. Shelly had the sinking suspicion that these two were hired by her competitors, her last employer even. People sent to pretend to buy a house. Surely, this pair were merely small-time actors hired at an hourly rate from Craigslist. They would laugh about it, ask about the showing, and pass around company memos at her expense.

She looked at the couple and tried to find something real, something tangible that would indicate they had money from a tech job, or maybe he was a passive income extraordinaire. Shelly didn't care about that, new money spent just as well as old money, and they were usually less picky about amenities or neighborhoods. No, new money cared about flashiness, especially in the bathrooms, and fiber optic internet.

Shelly found nothing that would indicate that the situation wasn't a hoax. Still, two could play at this game. She proceeded with the tour. The young couple marveled at the elegance as Shelly gave her best performance yet. The stage, an empty house, and this was her backdrop, her curtain and lights. So what if they weren't real, it was showtime all the same.

She stood in all the right places while presenting the rooms. She opened doors with ease, she even tapped with her fresh maroon fingernails as she casually mentioned the granite countertops and new appliances.

The seasoned real estate performer always ended in the kitchen. An old timer once taught her this tactic. Her mentor had since made enough money to drink himself silly. He said, "The kitchen is where the business occurs, remember that if nothing else." Shelly had known and believed, she had seen it work firsthand on countless occasions.

The couple's eyes were huge as they peered over the chrome and the convenience of everything. Lance helplessly opened the empty refrigerator, nodded as if he had no idea how it worked, what he would put in there, and took his place next to his girlfriend as the show demanded.

Shelly was in control, fake or not, this couple begged for her performance, her will. They wore the 3-D glasses as suggested and paid for the overpriced popcorn.

"Do you have financing? Are you pre-approved? What about an agent?" Shelly bombarded casually with a wince behind a fake, warm smile.

"Not yet. We…" Lance stammered at the adult questions.

"Oh that's fine, I can suggest a good lender that can help with that. What do you do?"

Shelly liked that question, it felt safe in her hands. It was a sure-fire shot across the bow of this Lance character and his unwed baby momma. Did they know that most houses get foreclosed on within the first year when bought by unwed couples? Clearly, they did not. Shelly was stopped in her tracks by his answer, his wrench in the machine's running.

"Computer programming," he responded while looking in the pantry.

She was losing their attention but needed to let them play like the children they were. Maybe this was for real. Perhaps they weren't hired by her competitors at all, even better.

Now, she had them right where she wanted. She could lead them to the sale easily from here, like an old pro hitting three under par, then taking a nap while waiting for the other golfers to finish the hole. There was that last swing to give them, but Shelly almost pulled back.

She thought over the details of the house, the trim, the master bath with double vanity. That would have to be enough, right? Still, they were already cued up and Shelly was in such good form. She pulled back her shoulders and swung away.

"Would you like to see the pool?" she asked with a sense of coy welcome.

"There's a pool?" Annette shrieked.

"Yeah, remember dear? I showed you the listing," Lance stood there as if he was going to draw down on Shelly, challenge her acting skills with a duel in the street.

She stared into his eyes and smiled with her pearly whites, past the matching maroon lipstick, puncturing his will. He turned with his girlfriend and gave in. Shelly pranced over to the sliding glass door, careful to open without breaking one of her fancy nail clackers. She let the couple go through first and take in the scene as she eagerly watched for their reaction.

"That's not a pool," Annette said with a child's disappointment.

"That is definitely going to need some work," Lance looked disgusted as he glanced about over the yard work, the future task of a real man.

"What do you mean?" Shelly looked out the sliding glass door to see.

There was no pool, no oasis glimmering in the sunshine of an open-house mid-morning. There was no ladder, no slide, no deep end, no robot, and no filter. There was no cabana, and no brightly-colored noodle left for effect. There was only an overgrown and underused backyard with withering fence and glutton vines. Flying bugs danced with glee over the high weeds and cracked patio.

Shelly tried to act casual, tried to say *Well, you could always put one in* or something professional that would quell the deep burning inside her stomach. Instead, her amateur-self ruined the façade and snatched at the listing on the counter, her own listing.

"What? But there was a pool, there had to be a pool. That was my final shot, my encore!"

Lance sensed her frustration, watched her as she tore at the edges of the computer printout and said, "It's ok really, I don't even like swimming."

"But I do, I thought you said there was a pool," Annette whined.

"Get out!" Shelly clenched her teeth. The vibration of the command was only heard by Lance.

"What?" he asked.

"I said, get out! Now!"

Lance went to ask again, but tiptoed over to his girlfriend and put his arm around her to guide her to the door.

"I know, by the way," Shelly said, making her hands

red while clutching the edges of the granite.

"You know what?" Lance asked over his shoulder.

"You're fake, this was all a show. You were hired to come here. I was good too, up until the last bit, up until the pool. You knew there wasn't a pool. That's how I know you're a fake. Who hired you?" Shelly asked, pointing at the pair with one of her sharp nails.

"What? No one. You are crazy. Come on Annette," Lance was at the door.

"I'll find out, I will. I'll find out and ruin one of *their* days, one of *their* showings. Tell that to whoever sent you, tell them I know what they're trying to do. Tell them I played along but I knew the whole time, all the way up until the pool."

Lance said nothing, but Shelly thought she detected a slight smile as he led his tearing girlfriend back to his beat-up Honda.

What a performance.

Shelly watched through the sparkling front window to see if they carried the act all the way to their car. She wanted to stand on the porch and yell more as they drove away. She went to the kitchen and grabbed her keys from her purse and ran out front. The couple sped away as Shelly popped the balloons attached to the open house sign which she pulled and threw in the yard next to the driveway. Satisfied with her efforts, she locked the door behind her, and threw herself on the faux leather. The staged couch in the living room of the house that was not hers provided a coolness that she was after. Her head whirled, then, nothing.

Three hours later and not a peep from the front door, Shelly awoke from a nap, a kind of midsummer daze. She drooled on herself, she drooled on the armrest and wondered if they would still take it back when the house was sold.

She looked at her watch and figured no one was coming. Good, she would have to call the lawn care company she used and inform them that they forgot to service the backyard. She could do that now, but there was something else.

"Damn!" Shelly whirled on her heels in the kitchen and almost fell over. She had to call the DJ for the party. She searched through her phone with her distracting nails for the saved contact, one of hundreds of contacts added and never managed over the years. She tried to remember what she saved it under.

There it was, she dialed and in the nicest tone she could muster, "Hi, yes, I'd like to book you for the 21st please? I have my daughter's birthday party and she said you were the best."

"Hold on a second ma'am, wow, that's close. I will have to check my calendar."

Instead of ruffling pages, Shelly could hear the

slight *click click* of phone noise on the other end as he checked his schedule. She examined her sleepy hair in the sliding glass door and waited.

"I am all booked up that weekend, perhaps another night?"

"No, no. She said you were the best and that night is already booked with the venue you see, and *we* need you instead. This is very important."

"Well, you should have called sooner ma'am. I am really sorry, but I usually get booked at least a month out."

"You don't understand dear, this is my daughter's sweet sixteen and she wants *you*, says *you* are the best."

"I do understand that ma'am, but I am all booked up. I'm sorry."

A slight pause, and Shelly fired her only weapon, "What are they paying you?"

"Excuse me?"

"What are they paying you, the other party? What is it, a wedding?"

"Yes, and they are paying me quite well, actually. They are paying me a thousand for this one night, only three hours too."

"I'll double it."

"What?"

"I'll double it, for four hours though."

"I don't know, they've already signed…"

"Fine, triple, paid up front, cash. You go ahead and hire one of your friends to do the other venue. You all use the same data files, no real discs anyway. Just buy some more speakers, hire one of your friends, and boom, you've expanded your business, all with the help of *me*."

"Um…I don't know what to say. Sure, why not?"

"Of course why not silly. See? Was that so hard? No. I will be over this afternoon to pay and sign, you work it out on your end."

"Yes, ah, yes ma'am! I will have the contract ready."

Shelly hung up the phone, completely satisfied that her deal making abilities were still intact. She had the small bother of a thought that Andrew would find out that he would be paying for her carelessness though.

With that future excuse in mind, she slid out of the glass door to investigate a minor detail that caught her eye. A small glint of metal shined in the light of the midafternoon which caused her feet to sink in the melting patio. There was a lock on the door to the side fence which gave access to the backyard, access needed by the landscapers.

Shelly stood there without purpose, not knowing what to do, where to go from here. She had no key.

Why did they think they could outsmart me? Whoever sent a snot-nosed actor to do a man's job...might as well have sent a toddler. No, I knew. They held each other's hands awkwardly, a dead giveaway.

Why even add that detail about a pregnancy? No college age bastard was aiming to please his pregnant girlfriend with a house. They had to know that a baby would cost more than a mortgage. That is if they wanted it to be more than a lump of skin and sadness.

Someone out beyond had sent this prank to me, but I was bored of sitting on the couch. Plus, I wanted to dazzle them. I wanted them to run off to whatever hellish monster sent them, tail between their legs, crying about what they saw.

It was all a gimmick anyway. Never about who I was selling to. It was about the house I was selling. Everything was choreographed from the tapping on the granite to the final room. It wasn't about them.

It was as much about them as a movie was about the people watching it. No. They were just passengers. I was their bus. Once we ended in the kitchen, they'd admit everything. I knew they would.

They took in tiny details that they'd been told to observe. The water pressure of the faucets, which no one ever cared about. Who would care about such trivial nonsense? Who cared how fast the faucets were?

Everything I did, as the entertainer, as the driver, as the performer, was about accenting the gleam. The shininess of the faucet far outweighed how fast you could wash your hands. If they cared so much about how fast they could wash their hands, and they didn't care how nice the faucet looked, then they should have considered a farm house. They could have a rusty metal tube with a rough metal handle on a square of white concrete in a corn field. It sure as hell would have been faster than the shiny chrome faucet.

I wanted to scream at them about how a home was never about how effective appliances were. It wasn't even about practicality. The nicest homes that I had shown had beautiful crystal chandeliers. It was perfect, but it served no purpose and it took a team of fourteen people to clean. A status symbol. A grand staircase wasn't about leaving the room open, no. It was a huge atrocity that took up far too much space. A huge staircase was about how grand it appeared to guests.

The house was in an up and coming development area, and it was a shiny diamond amongst a sea of low-income garbage. It was all a show, because everything was a show. If things were important based on their purpose, then basketball players wouldn't make money.

This hot shot punk probably wore a suit to his first interview, but he wasn't in one now. He was in a polo and khakis. The green grass was created to get rid of the blight of yellow dirt. Grass caused more problems than it solved. Landscaping companies made so much money because we want our grass to be greener. We pay them for style. We waste water because it looks good.

They were a pretty couple though, and almost convincing. Except she was out of his league. Her painted on beauty was clearly the source of his discomfort. She wasn't pregnant.

Who were my competitors kidding? They knew that I was a mother of two, so why would they think this would be convincing to me?

I danced effortlessly from room to room, answering his ignorant questions. Finally, I felt like everything was going perfect, and for once, I was a one-woman belle of the ball.

They didn't seem impressed, but that made sense. They weren't here to buy a house. They were children getting paid for a job. If I had access to good actors, I may have considered doing the same.

Still, I wanted them to be dazzled. I wanted them to like the house, at least then someone would like it. As of now, it was an outrageously expensive house amongst crap. It was basically a steak in a burger joint.

But I saw her tan lines and I went for it. I crouched in the tall grass, and I pounced onto the sliding door. It opened into the beating white sun, and the pool. Except there wasn't a pool. It broke everything. My heart crumbled like broken glass into my stomach. There wasn't room for a pool. There wasn't even a nice yard.

Beyond the shimmering glass of the beautiful exterior, the house was just as crappy as the others. It was just a hat on an ugly dog. It was a façade. It was a fake. I wanted this house to be the one that I sold. I wanted it to be my only deal, but they knew.

After I rested, trying to get over the fact that everything was a lie, I glimpsed a beacon of hope. Deep inside the rugged terrain of the backyard, there was a shimmering lock, gleaming in the lie. It was set behind a shrub, unassuming. I pulled the lock, but it was firmly in place. Even though the door wasn't very high, I couldn't let the landscapers in, and I still felt trapped. I was the one who was locked up. I tapped the door, trying to get the attention of a lock picking expert, but no one came.

No one was going to come. This was the place where everyone hid their biggest secret. The house's secret was that it didn't have a pool, or even a backyard. People were like that. I knew it. I could see through their intent. We were all lonely inside, waiting to swim in our warm pool of lies.

Integrity was nothing, and being human was being selfish. That idea was the only reason I could stay in business, if you could call it a business. I turned back towards the sliding glass door. I saw my reflection, and I imagined Julie standing behind me, getting ready to jump into the non-existent pool. She vanished into the *dirt, and I felt my breath leave my lungs. Where was she going? What was she trying to do?*

I crawled over to the patch of dirt where she had vanished, and I pulled the weeds out of the way. It took everything inside me, but I snapped my nails off and started digging. I clawed at the ground, gouging out huge chunks of dirt. No matter how much I dug, I couldn't see her.

"Julie!" But she didn't answer. I kept digging, knowing that she was sinking by the minute. My hope was that the party would serve as a lighthouse for her to drift back to me, but I was already off to a bad start. If the party didn't go well, she would never get out of the ground. I'd lose her forever.

"Julie!" I screamed again, but still no answer. My only choice was to keep digging, until the dirt wedged under my fingernails which turned to blood and my fingers went numb. Even then, I continued to dig. She was all I had. My business was broken, I was ridiculed, and my husband was losing interest in me. Andy would always love me, but he would learn better.

"Julie!" I slammed my hand into the ground, trying to wake her, but she was gone. She was so far gone. The party was my life raft. I was adrift in the sea, and she was a tiny boat going somewhere great. I had one last shot.

I smiled as I looked down at my bloody hands, remembering her tiny hands when she was born. There was a streak of blood up her arm, but it didn't bother me. Her hand was warm in mine. I kept smiling until tears fell into the hole I had dug.

As I continued crying, the warmth from her hand started to vanish and all I had was an empty feeling in my chest. I needed to buckle down. "Deep breath. Deep breath." The DJ was right, I couldn't plan things only a few weeks in advance.

I gripped the dirt and wiped the blood. Before I left the backyard, I took one last fleeting glance at the lock. It still couldn't keep me in. Tomorrow, I would come back with bolt cutters to let the landscapers do their job. I'd make sure they cleaned up the backyard nicely. And I'd paint the chipping fence, and even though it wouldn't have a pool, it would still be beautiful.

After all that was complete, I'd host another open house, and I would sell it to the first people who came in. No buts about it. I'd turn around, take that money, and buy my beautiful baby something she deserved, and she would finally love me again.

I locked my legs and stood tall, wiping dirty tears from my eyes. If I kept this attitude up, I could conquer the world. That warm feeling appeared back in my hand and I smiled. I strode back into the house, across the foyer, grabbed the sign from the yard, and threw it in my car.

Everything will work out, it's quintessential.

CHAPTER Ten

At the bank, Shelly marked the check *Cash* and wrote in the memo *For Party*. "Hundreds please," she said, handing the signed check to the teller.

Looking around, she noticed some college students, a vet arguing over his social security check, and a mousy thirty something in thrift store clothing. She thought about the other banks in town and wondered if their clientele could draw three grand, just like that. None of these people around her could. As the teller handed her the envelope with new, flat bills, she thought about cashing in all of their accounts right there and moving to a more suitable establishment that understood the need for self-image for its customers.

Despite the terrible showing at the open house and those punk kids, Shelly felt better carrying all that cash in her purse, and driving her Mercedes to the DJ's hangout. A woman of power, determination. A woman with money, out in the world, getting things done.

She had to get to the DJ before he set out for a gig. He told her to meet him at his apartment garage where he would be loading his gear. He would have the contract ready for her to sign. The thought of going to an apartment complex with a wad of cash made her feel a little dangerous and excited.

The last time she lived in an apartment was when she and Andrew were first married. He was just starting out and all they could afford was a one bedroom that they barely furnished. Times were different then, her expectations were less chaotic. They were simple. She was a wife first, and soon to be mother second. That was all. Her calling, her duty. What happened?

She thumbed for the garage number on her phone and noted that hers was in fact the only Mercedes in the parking lot, check. The complex was fairly new and the hot sun mirrored off the windows and the glazed railings to the three-story walk-ups. While still searching on her phone for the garage number, Shelly nearly ran into a large white van with the magnetic stickers for "Sound City Performance". She complimented in her mind the cute music notes and overall design of the words and logo. Rather than search for parking, she stopped her car right there in front of another garage and got out.

"Hello?" Shelly could hear someone hefting

equipment into the van. The tire weight sagged and she could see work boots on the ramp but no head. She clutched her purse with the cash and looked around. "Hello?"

"Yes, hello miss, can I help you?" She heard from inside the garage.

"I'm here to sign a contract and pay. We spoke on the phone, I'm Shelly."

"Shelly Dougherty, the real estate agent, of course," the man jumped down from the ramp. "I've been expecting you. I have your contract right here. I'm Wesley."

Shelly stopped short. On the phone, she thought she was talking to a college student or a zit-faced kid. That made bullying around and bribery a lot easier. In person, Wesley was a handsome man in his mid-thirties with purposeful graying above the ears and a thick head of sandy blonde hair. He wiped his hand and face on a handkerchief from his torn jean pocket and offered her his strength. She peered with curiosity at his sweaty, grey t-shirt and three-day stubble and offered her own hand.

"I'm glad you could meet me on such short notice," was all she could muster. She could smell him. Sweat mixed with some kind of cologne, a classic she remembered from her childhood. She looked at his toned forearms, his broad chest as she stepped closer with caution into the hot garage. There were lights, a few work benches, and a portable air conditioner, but most of the contents were already loaded into the van. She turned her body toward the ramp and music equipment.

"Oh yes, sorry about that Shelly. I had to meet you here because I have a gig an hour away and I had to get things loaded up to go," Wesley stood next to the cool air blowing in and took gulps of water from an ice-filled gym bottle. "Duty calls," he chuckled over water, "but, I have your contract right here. I already signed. You were very persistent."

"Well, it's my daughter's sixteenth birthday and I just waited too long for-"

"That's fine Shelly, really. I stay so busy too, I understand." He handed her a one-page contract for the event and pulled a pen out of his shirt pocket.

Shelly focused on his chest where the pen came from, and his lightly freckled, glazed with sweat forearm. *He cut her off, how could he do that?* She took the contract and pen, tried to look over the words but couldn't help notice his strong legs as he hefted the last speaker pedestal into the van. He clasps his hard hand around, closing the cold metal doors with a sound that she expected but that still made her jump on the inside.

She pretended to read the contract. Instead, she checked the date, signed and handed it back over. She looked into his grey eyes and boyish smile as he took the paper and set it carefully on a workbench under a light.

"I'm just going to take a picture and send it to you, no copier in here," he chuckled again. That laugh.

"That's fine," she responded. All business. Keep it all business. But something inside of her was beginning to burn, to take shape.

That laugh made her want to fall over and die. He was so nonchalant, so smooth with his simple words. He acted as if he didn't have a care in the world, didn't care that he was in an apartment complex, like it was a matter of course. She looked again at his newer white van and magnet decals and wondered how much he made. She thought about asking but he likely didn't care. *Just enough to keep going*. That's what he would say to her if she asked, but she wouldn't, she knew. She saw old turntables, relics of the past, and record stacks. She sensed that he loved his job. What a wonder to love your job. To turn a hobby into a profession.

"There, all set. Now, we are bound. I got the song list from your daughter already and I will be sure to accommodate. I have a good mix already planned for her. I know how stressful these parties can be, but you are all set here. You'll see that I marked it as *paid*," Wesley gazed into her eyes and she melted from either the heat or his physique. He gave off an expectant smile.

"Oh right," Shelly fumbled uncontrollably in her purse for the envelope. *Where?* So many things. There. She handed it to him with great pride but he handled it like a piece of junk mail. Wesley disappeared behind a rack of old records.

She had to get back control and paying was the first step. She had felt so out of control the past few days and she thought that she had pinned this man using triple the pay, but that wasn't so. Sure, he agreed to her demands after she offered the money and he would show up on time, but she didn't have control over him now, couldn't. He had somewhere else to be, someone else to entertain. Why was it so hard for her? Look at him, he had much to be thankful for and a cruising attitude. What about her? What about her needs? Her dreams? Why so difficult? He knew what he was doing, she did not. She needed to regain control, to take back her life that had been whirling. She needed power. How?

"Thank you so much for your business. Again, I'm sorry about having to meet you here but I have to get cleaned up and on the road to the next gig, so…" His voice trailed and this time, she cut him off with a sound, a sharp shhh or a word of command with a finger held to his chest.

She pushed him back, testing his hard muscles in an authoritative way. He only stepped back with the pressure and smiled a strange, knowing smile with those white teeth and those eyes of calm avoidance of life's misery.

She turned to go, instead she gave a stubborn grin right back at him and punched the garage door button. As it closed, she stood there staring at him, daring him to run. Next to that button were the lights. With the gesture of a girl having a fit, she clicked that switch as well for good measure. She carefully stepped with heels only, no eyes, on the hard pavement in the dark. His smell got stronger until she groped the warm, solid figure that said nothing. He obeyed her commands as she breathed on his stubbled cheek.

He groped back. He took his time.

Shelly looked at him as the garage door opened, searching for a sense of defeat in his eyes. They had fumbled in the dark, had played a game that she started. She had won. He said nothing, she had demanded it earlier. He only stood there with a one-arm wave, hair chaotic from her touch, clothes disturbed. She put on her sunglasses and left him there with that smile.

She marched into the blinding sun after the dark session and realized her car was still running. How long? She didn't know, didn't care. Long enough to feel him pulsing inside of her and what he left was still there when she opened her door and sat down. Good, she wanted that reminder of her big win of the day. No guilt, not for winners. Not yet.

She wanted to keep his sweat for as long as she could, but would have to go home soon. *What would Andrew think? What would Andrew do?* No time for that. There were plans, there were always plans. They would go on without her if she didn't show. Just another Saturday without mom.

Shelly drove on without looking back. She came to a stoplight and adjusted her mirror to face herself. She reapplied her lipstick and fixed her ravished hair. How beautiful. How sexy. She gave a loud giggle at herself as she pursed her lips in the mirror. How powerful she was, how seductive. The car behind her beeped as the light had already turned. Shelly punched the gas on her little Mercedes and raced back to reality.

CHAPTER Eleven

The Dougherty house and surrounding neighborhood was quiet for a Friday night. Andrew had knocked off of work early to swim with Andy. With no Friday evening appointments, a new rule asked by Andrew, and Julie's party the next day, things were uncomfortably calm. Shelly had only a showing Saturday morning and an open house to worry about Sunday. All was well. Even the neighborhood contained within its roundabouts and perfect grass, a quiet contentment that prolonged as the heat subsided.

Shelly remained in her business attire, poised on the breakfast bar with her Cosmo. A cup of easy sweet tea from the fridge marked a circular puddle on the granite countertop next to the magazine. She listlessly flipped through the pages as a distraction. She was waiting for her boys to get done swimming so they could all decide what to do about dinner.

The last week or so ran along without incident. Shelly fielded more calls from buyers and sellers alike, but still had yet to sell a property. This was expected. She warned herself before starting this business that it would take time, but the prospect of getting a quick sale fast and early was so intoxicating that she forgot her own cautions. If the Tudor had not given her such a shake of early excitement, she would be plugging along as usual, knowing that her efforts would pay off in the long run.

That, and the messy situation with Wesley, gave her something to dwell upon. But he wouldn't tell, and neither would she. When she returned home from that day at the garage, she had simply given the excuse that the house she was showing was without air and quickly showered upstairs. She kept her distance, knowing that men could smell such things, subconsciously or not. She and Andrew had not made love since then, too busy. This allowed her even less remorse for her guilty encounter with the DJ.

Shelly thought that maybe Andrew wanted her the night before when they were going over last-minute party arrangements. He had been casual in the Andrew way, flirty even. She checked off her small to-do list and he rattled off everything else. Nina had really helped him out with the decorations, the favors, and the food. Shelly wanted to thank Nina but that would have to wait. She hadn't seen her since the pool on the debut day of Quintessential Realty. Had she been there the whole time?

Life was so busy and she felt like she was treading water, except for that afternoon in the garage. There, she felt like a true winner, a doer with satisfaction. She wondered how Wesley felt as she let her eyes glaze over the bright pages and perfect skin tones in the magazine. She didn't care, and it was likely that he didn't either, or that he would cause any kind of scene at a paid gig when he saw her again. Professionalism prevails once again.

With that thought in mind, she heard the boys come in from the pool. They brought the heat with them as Andrew dried his face with a towel around his neck. He wore a Hawaiian shirt and his chest hair gleamed from his tanned skin as he cracked open a beer from the fridge. Andy grabbed something from the pantry and ran upstairs.

"Hi mom! Bye mom!"

She waved back like in a beauty pageant.

"He's getting really good out there. He can swim across the whole pool underwater," Andrew said, giving a kiss and a hug between gulps.

"Oh? He must have a good teacher," she could smell the sunscreen and chlorine mix with his scent as she grabbed the back of him and tasted sweet beer. He looked good in the summer, manly even.

"Reading that garbage again, are ya?" He asked, searching the fridge for food.

"Not really, kind of just sitting here. I was going to join you but I only managed to take off my heels," she looked down at her stuffy blouse and her ironed pants. She wished that Andrew would stop fooling around and just take off her clothes for her, take her right there in the kitchen. Then, she remembered the joys of parenthood caused by previous encounters of the like. She heard Andy running around upstairs, probably throwing his wet trunks on the carpet and leaving robot dinosaurs in the hallway.

"The venue is all set up, took care of that this morning. I got the car, it's parked in the back so nobody can take a peak," Andrew said past the crunching of chips.

"I thought you only had this afternoon off?"

"Couldn't, too much to do, needed the whole day. Nina was a big help though, and Andy checked a few of the balloons to see if they could pop. Everything's good, all set now. Hey, why did the DJ cost so much?"

"He was already booked, but that's who she wanted. Sorry. Hey, where is Julie?" she asked, attempting to change the subject.

"Says she's out at the movies, then the mall. Don't know right now. Says she's sleeping over at her friend Tina's house tonight. Can't keep track."

Shelly could tell that he was a little irritated by being the one responsible for their daughter. She would always talk to her father on her phone, but not her. Shelly wondered why.

"Oh, ok. Well, anything I need to get? Anything you need me to do?" she asked with a thread of guilt in her voice.

"No, like I said, it's all set. We took care of it."

Shelly watched as her husband finished making his sandwich. As he headed out to the back patio, she realized he was mad about something. Sure, this would pass along with the actual party and many more, but Shelly knew that if she continued in a constant state of work, the two of them would grow all the more distant.

She thought about changing upstairs and joining her husband on the patio, but his coldness made her go soft. All she really wanted to do was go away on another vacation. Maybe she would plan a surprise trip for them to take after the party. She could ask Andrew to take certain days off and they could go to that cabin in the woods where little Andy was conceived. She started to look on her phone for reservations but couldn't remember the name of the cabins. It was in the Great Smoky Mountains and Andrew loved it there, but that was all she could remember. Where had they gone? She tossed her phone with a chunk on the kitchen counter, threw the Cosmo in the trash and headed upstairs.

"Honey. Honey, someone's at the door. Honey, our phones are ringing. Honey!" Shelly shook her husband awake. When had she gone to sleep? When did she settle for the night? He was a known hard-sleeper. As she did, she noticed that her work clothes were still on. Had she been out that long? Andrew had a half-empty beer on the nightstand and the TV was still playing episode after episode of Andrew's stupid show. But the doorbell...and the phones. "Honey!" She shook him. His reality came into focus and he looked around the room, then back at her.

"What...what's wrong?" He maintained the same irritated tone with her as before. He sat straight up with another doorbell ring.

"Someone's at the door," she repeated, ripping the covers off her husband. He stood straight up and started for the stairs. "Wait, your robe," Shelly got up too, grabbing the matching set and handing over his. She put her own robe on over her clothes. It all somehow felt safer that way.

Whoever was at the door started banging instead.

"I'm coming, I'm coming," Andrew grew more awake with the second repetition of the words.

Shelly stood at the top of the stairs, clasping the warm robe around her business attire. Surprised she had slept that long, she forgot to take out her small hoop earrings and her ears ached with the pressure. She undid them and put them in the robe pocket. Andrew turned the porch light on and opened the door.

"Mr. Dougherty?"

"Yes? Julie! What happened?"

"Oh Daddy, I'm so sorry!"

Shelly saw the dark blue uniform and Julie hugging her father in the doorway. She wanted to interject, but remained frozen at the top of the stairs, a nonexistent gate guard held her there.

"Mr. Dougherty, Julia here was found at a house party where there was copious amounts of alcohol, with underage drinking. We are going to investigate the house and the parents of the residence. I will call on you for any information you can give in the morning. That's all for now though, we have a lot of kids to take home."

"Ok, alright officer, thank you," Andrew closed the door, still holding Julia.

"Daddy, I didn't drink anything, I swear!" Shelly could hear a drunk and whiney little girl in there somewhere.

"There, there now, we'll talk about it in the morning," Andrew said, looking up at his wife.

As commanded with his eyes, Shelly carefully walked down the carpeted stairs.

"Let's get you some water honey, I'll bet you're

thirsty," she said, taking Julia's hand and shoulder. She led her daughter to the kitchen and filled a cup from the door, no ice.

Julia moaned as she took a few sips with the help of her mother. Her mascara ran down her cheeks as Shelly remembered her little girl banging her knee on a slide, way back when.

With that fond memory came another kind of moan, a guttural one, as Julia tried to hold back the wretch. Shelly quickly led her daughter into the half-bath under the stairs, held the girl's hair back, and tried not to puke herself.

"What did you have?" Shelly asked.

"They called it *Jungle Juice,*" Julie said between heaves.

Shelly could smell the alcohol coming from her daughter's pores. Andrew paced about the kitchen, itching his scalp, trying to control his anger.

After five minutes of horrible repetition and waiting, Shelly led Julia to the comfort and darkness of the living room sofa. She motioned for more water from Andrew and fed her baby girl some needed hydration.

"There, there," Shelly said, stroking her face with a washcloth, cleaning like she did when her little girl was a baby. Shelly covered up the scantily clad fifteen-year-old with a blanket and used her lap as a pillow. "You have to get your water dear and rest up. After all, you've got a party tomorrow." She looked at Andrew as she spoke the words, flat-faced and in defiance. He exhaled loudly with that thought.

"I'm so sorry Daddy, I'm so..." And she was gone. A tiny smile set upon her face past tears of runny mascara and regret.

After a while, with some familiar glances between the couple as during the baby years, Andrew tiptoed, leaving mother and daughter downstairs to rest.

"No jungle juice though, not at my baby girl's party. No, that wouldn't do, now would it?" Julie repeated in a cooing voice as if to baby Julie. She continued to stroke her daughter's hair and didn't fall asleep herself until just before dawn.

MARC D. CREPEAUX & A.M. HOUNCHELL

CHAPTER Twelve

"Are we just going to pretend like nothing even happened?" Andrew asked while putting on his pants.

"No, but what do you want to do exactly? Cancel the party? We've spent nearly ten grand, plus the car. Should we just tell everyone that they can't come? What about all the trouble we've gone through?" Shelly smirked on the inside, the *trouble* she had gone through with the DJ was nothing.

"Yes, yes. I know all this," Andrew bobbed his head in exaggerated agreement, the way he did when he was overwhelmed by an argument and wanted to play devil's advocate just the same. "But, caught drinking? At this age? If we go on like nothing happened, what kind of message will that send?"

"So, we'll play nice for today, then ground her after.

She can get the new car, but won't be able to drive it right away." Shelly undressed, finally out of her business attire from nearly twenty-four hours prior. Her husband, now fully dressed, just gawked at her as she sat there naked on the bed with her legs crossed, finally comfortable. She dared him to argue further.

The party was not only for Julia, it was a status check for their household, their hard work, and their name. Shelly wanted to play the good parent for once, and coming down hard on Julie at this time would only mean more strife.

"You know she organized the party, right?" Andrew stated in defiance, trying not to stare, trying not to be swayed from his position by his wife as she lightly stroked her legs and arms. Shelly was aiming for a hot, overdue shower, not sex, but Andrew didn't know that.

"I'm not surprised. She does have a certain skill set," Shelly's response was flat, uncaring as she busied herself with her skin. Her soft hands moved about her neck and shoulders as she began massaging them herself.

"You seem proud? I am so confused," Andrew said. He began folding towels, a distraction from the distraction.

"In a way, I am. She has a certain knack for organizing people. When today is over, we will have to help her channel that energy."

"*We?* You mean *me?* You're never here." Andrew's

voice raised, he looked at the bedroom door then it lowered to a hiss. "I'm the one always monitoring, always knowing where she is, who she's with. It's exhausting, Shel." He sat on the bed next to her, giving in. He didn't have the energy for a fight, hardly ever did. With this action, they became teammates once again.

Andrew tried with that shot, but Shelly maintained control. She always had control, only she sometimes forgot. She looked at his pants. Despite the conflict, the towel folding, and the fate of their world, he was still a man. He had no control. She wanted to grab him by his helm there, on the bed, but she waited. The matter wasn't completely settled. Andrew was still in strife mode. She put her hand on his shoulder and compared it to Wesley's. It wasn't as strong, not as cut, but it was hers, all hers. His skin was tanned and muscles were toned from summer activities.

"We can settle this after the party. We can go hard on her, ground her, and lecture her to death if we want. We can give her the car but take away the keys. I will try and spend less time on the houses, maybe even quit *Quintessential Realty*."

"What? Why?" Andrew turned and asked. He responded with ease to her shoulder rub but jumped a little at that thought.

"It's taking a toll on the family." If she admitted that fact openly, and he gave in, she would have him where she wanted.

"Yeah, but…it's your dream."

"I know, but I'm failing."

"You're not *failing*, it will just take time. Give it a little more time, six months. If in six months, you can't afford to hire a few more agents and work less, then quit. Heck, sell it if you can. *Okay?*"

She had him right where she wanted him. She just bought herself six months of freedom. Six months to hit the ground running with no consequences because of what he just said. Such a good boy.

"Okay, no, you're right," Shelly said, pretending to contemplate his wise words.

The conflict was over. All matters were settled in accordance with…Wait, one more action to seal up the agreements. The sound of the judge's gavel needed to be heard throughout the *entire* courtroom. She pushed her husband back on the bed, methodically took off his pants, and climbed over his will.

Andrew said nothing. He only stared in awe at her great power and beauty.

CHAPTER Thirteen

The Daugherty family arrived arm in arm to the birthday party, a half hour before the celebration was to begin. Andrew had already been there to make final preparations with Nina who had gone back to get her family. The new car was out front and a big matching bow took over most of the hood. Julia tried to act surprised but the previous night's incident and the known expectations of her day quelled some of the spark. Still, there were tears of joy all around. Even little Andy's eyes were large when he sat in the backseat of his big sister's new car.

As the family walked inside, they were awestruck with the abundance. A whole row of catered food trays were covered and steaming in the overhead, sparkling lights. Each table had matching sets of dishware, hats, and other party favors in individual bags. The tablecloths all matched her sweet sixteen car's color, and the chairs and tables lined the inner wall left plenty of room for a dancefloor.

The DJ began playing low as the royal family entered. Shelly refused to make eye contact but noted that Wesley was dressed in a smart, white suit and thin tie for the occasion. The family swarmed around, checking the signature plates and dishes, and Shelly stopped little Andy from opening one of the gift bags. There was a table where the massive cake would go, along with a side table for the gifts. Shelly noted that the table for the gifts was likely too small, considering the guest list was more than thirty people.

A half hour passed and they waited. Wesley played on, song after song. The family began milling about the door, peering outside, checking their phones.

"No one is answering me, I sent out a mass text," Julia said, attempting to remain calm.

"It's fine honey, maybe everyone's running a little late is all." Shelly put her arm on Julia who skirted away. She looked at her daughter and compared her with the crying baby the night before. Now, she looked so mature, all made-up, and so serious.

Nina walked in all smiles and hugged Shelly. Everyone was quiet with expectation.

"Gary and the kids will be along shortly. Everyone

is dragging," Nina said to the room. Andrew just nodded. His forehead began to shrink. He gave in a little and sat by the door. Both women could see that the expectation was taking its toll on the man who largely planned the event.

Julia's phone began to chime a sparkly sound. One, then another, then another. The birthday girl couldn't swipe fast enough. One after another, *chime, chime, chime*. That hopeful sound over and over and above the room, above Wesley's half-volume music, hovering above their hopes. *Chime, chime, chime.*

"*Can't come*. Mom, that's what they're all saying. *Can't come, grounded. Can't come, Can't come, Happy Birthday!, Sorry, Can't come, grounded. Can't come, grounded. Can't come, Can't come, Happy Birthday! Sorry, Can't come.* "Mom! What is happening? Why can't anyone come? Why?" *Chime, chime, chime.* "Mom! Answer me! Mom!" Julia screamed at her mother.

Shelly just stood there and gawked at her child's worried face. She began to bob her head, reacting to the *chime, chime, chime* of her daughter's phone.

"It's all my fault," Julia fell to her knees and began to weep. "It's all my fault. The party last night, I made it happen. I invited them *all*. I mixed the drinks. I got them *all* there. All *my fault* mother, all *my fault*."

Chime, chime, chime.

The music stopped. Shelly looked back at Wesley. He was frozen. His headphones were still on, he still wore the suit, but he was frozen. He looked capable and ready to push the next song button, but there was no sound.

Andrew picked Julia up as if she were a toddler and made for the door. Before leaving, he gave Shelly a hard look and motioned for Andy to follow. The boy ran out too and disappeared.

Julia's phone remained on the floor. *Chime, chime, chime.*

Shelly whirled on her heels, her party dress swayed in slow motion. The steam above the food remained motionless, not dissipating as it should. Shelly felt a pain inside her belly, such burning pain and fire.

She looked down, blood was everywhere, running down her party dress. She looked at her arms and felt happy burning, her arms were scratched beyond belief, over and over. Scars upon scabs upon scars. Blood ran down her legs and pooled in her heels, some gathering on the floor where she stamped with her spikes into the thick red dark. Nina remained frozen but staring at her with a look of deep concern stamped on her pretty face.

Shelly touched the blood on her stomach, moved her hands in front of her eyes, and wiped the warmth on her cheeks. She scratched over the clawing on her arms, testing her own will, feeling the pleasure.

She marched over to the food. One by one, she turned over dish after dish, kicking and punching the hotplates and utensils. Food splattered and some of it joined the trail of blood that followed her, that pooled around her. The blood that came from her own stomach.

Shelly toppled tables and chairs, the speakers, the favors, and the weighted balloons. She scratched her arms, her face, she used broken glass to etch messages into the walls and floor. The same shards were tested on her skin, symbols drawn in blood on her legs and feet.

She whirled about the room as a tornado, leaving nothing beautiful behind, nothing without blood, nothing undisturbed. Her hands and arms burned from the work. She began to lose her breath as she fought back from the weakness. She stormed about, nothing without blood, nothing without hate, nothing without devil marks.

Then, she collapsed on the floor, bobbed and shook, thumbing her wounds.

Shelly's lungs burned and she could feel that wretched sense of life in her veins, in the heaving of her lungs. Oh, how she hated that feeling, how she wished it was never there, wished it would go away. She caught her breath and started scratching again, digging her perfect nails into her bloody and scabbed arms. *Why wouldn't they just fall off? Why wouldn't they die?*

Nina broke her spell, appeared from her frozen state by her side. She spoke in soft tones, came from a white, safe place. *What was she saying?* So nice, she sounded so nice and pleasant in that way. Such a good friend. Shelly felt a prick. Her arms and legs became lifeless. *Safe place.* She saw her legs protruding out in front of her, blood all over them and her dress.

A gown? No, it was too short and the floor was too cold. *Where was the music? Where was Wesley?*

She felt a hard fabric on her arms. *Rough cloth, pressured hands, kind words.* Nina, those were Nina's kind words. She would know what to do. She said it all the time. Nina could help, had helped. Nina was helping now with her kind words and hard touch. She needed that hard touch from her *friend* and those kind words that would help her with Julie and Andrew, and little Andy. *Yes. Such a good friend.*

Then, another safe, happy phrase rolled past her ears. Nina had such a smooth voice, could fix anything.

Another prick in the arm.

Then, nothing.

The party ended, I don't remember how. I found myself back in my office, staring at the white walls. I would have called Julie, but I knew she wouldn't answer. No. She couldn't answer. Preoccupied by the overwhelming disaster.

I wished that I could go to her, but my door was blocked by hundreds of crows. They set cawing at the door to Quintessential Realty, waiting for the crumbs of my decaying business. They wanted my blood too, I could see it in their black eyes.

They spiraled above in dark clouds, leaving my business under the darkened sky. They had seen my ad. Birds had houses. They needed to know how cold it was. They needed to know when to fly south for the winter.

I waited by the window for the birds to leave, but they didn't. They perched in trees, waiting for me to take flight too. If I wasn't so afraid, I may have joined. The bars on the windows were far too thick to fit my human head through.

Once, a bird landed on the windowsill, I grabbed it by the neck and twisted it off. It pulsed blood onto the ground, but the head smiled at me. I needed the birds and the people to know that I was trapped. Must get out a message.

I pressed my pinky into the neck of the bird, coating it in blood.

Help.

A simple suggestion. Anyone would misunderstand. I sat there staring at the fragments of phone and alternating to the off-white wall. I rehearsed my next appointments.

I slept.

Then, I heard an ice cream truck. It stopped in front of my office, and a man, dressed in white approached the window.

"Beef or chicken?" He said.

"Ice cream."

"You know we don't have that." Impossibly, the man pushed his hand through the window to hand me a tray.

"This isn't ice cream."

"It never is." Then the man escaped back to his ice cream truck.

The window watching the bright green grass wave in the sun. It was a comical green against the yellow backdrop of the desert.

I took the plate off of the inside window sill. The ice cream truck was gone, but I had something to eat. I sat in my chair, facing the door and the cawing of crows. I threw the plate of chicken as hard as I could in defiance to the crows. They weren't going to let me leave my office.

"Psst," a voice muttered from inside the wall.

"Psst," I said back. Nobody was around, except for the black feathers. They screeched out of place, revealing the front door to my house.

Knock! Knock! I found myself knocking without meaning to, without moving really. Andrew answered.

"I see you finally got dinner finished," he said, ripping the tray from my hand. He threw it on the ground and swiped the dirty mixed remnants into a bowl. "Made your favorite."

It was my favorite. I plunged a spoon deep into the mixed concoction and found myself in pure bliss. The dust off the floor mixed effortlessly with the salty chicken.

"How's Julie?"

"Ask her yourself." Julie stepped from behind a lamp, and she shattered to the ground.

"I'm never going to forgive you," she said.

"I'm your mother."

"Not anymore."

My face appeared in the lamp, with her in a million pieces making me feel insignificant and dull.

"Guess we don't need you anymore," Andrew said.

"Wait! Julie! I'm sorry. I didn't mean for anything bad to happen to you." It didn't matter. She was separated from me by hundreds of cold shoulders and thousands of texts. It was a track that looped around the world fifty times. No matter how fast I ran, it felt like I never went anywhere. One-bedroom apartment, simple pleasure. New wife, soon to be mother.

"Wish I was sorry." Andrew slammed the door, and it exploded out of my office. That cheating bastard had

bought that lamp earlier in the week. I took a bite from the mixed bowl of garbage and chicken fat from the floor.

I sat in my office waiting for the crows to lighten up. I waited for them to take flight, but they were useless. They perched in corners outside, watching with unblinking eyes. They weren't going to stop watching, and I was never going to be able to leave.

"Psst," I heard again. The door tilted to one side, melting itself into the wall. Another uncontrollable knock knock pressed itself from my knuckles to the wood.

"Hello?" Julie called out.

"Julie. I love you so much!"

"How can I help you?"

"I'm your mother!"

"I don't have a mother."

The final syllable in mother struck me like a bullet. It smashed through my chest and sent me falling backwards. I fell and fell until I was laying at the bottom of a grave. Julie was still standing in the doorway above, watching me.

"This is what happens to dead weight." She shoveled dirt into the hole.

I tried clawing my way out. She continued until dirt filled my nostrils and caked around my eyes. The ghost of my baby girl was still in my arms, writhing in pain. I couldn't feed her from my nipple or a bottle. Instead, she was shrinking away from me.

I tried clutching her to my world, but she continued getting smaller and smaller. She was the size of a bean. Her cry was impossibly loud, but I couldn't feed her or soothe her. I was a failure.

The size of a bean, I could plant her in the ground. I tried just that, but I could hear her cry through the dirt, too. Her screaming came through the dirt, glass, and time. No matter how much I tried, I'd always be a terrible mother.

The tears falling from my face turned black against the dusty grey ground. For a moment, I saw a flicker of green in there. Julie's voice became louder through the floor, and I realized she was nourished by my salt. I just needed more crying to bring her back.

I pushed my fingers into my right eye, until the pain swelled in my stomach. Blood pushed from the socket, dripping onto the black spot on the ground. If I could just give her more, she could sprout back.

"Please! Please! Come back! I love you. I need you." Blood washed over my eyes and face, tinting my vision red with rust and dirt. I let it cake and picked at it again like a crow.

"Mom?" Julie's voice was light like the wind through a hole in a fence.

"We can fix your birthday! We can fix it." I wiped the blood out of my eyes, and my office had transformed into puffy white walls and a solid concrete slab. My blood and tears were pooled on the floor with bits of skin that held my eye together.

"No. I don't want this. Take me back to my daughter. Take me back. Take me back!" I slammed my bloody fist into the wall. Someone needed to notice.

I focused my eyes on the door as the locks screeched. I put myself into a crouching position, ready to take another bite out of someone's neck. The Man in White on the other side of the steel door was holding a long syringe.

"Shelly, calm down."

I let out a low growl.

"I swear to God, if you bite me again."

I leaped towards him, and he smashed the needle into my chest. My teeth wrapped around his arm, but before I could pull his flesh from him, everything turned black.

I woke up, lathered in cold sweat, lying next to Andrew. It had been a dream. It all felt so real.

"Andrew?" I put my hand on his chest, feeling his warm skin and his coarse hair. This felt better.

"What…" he said, trailing off, back to sleep.

"I had a nightmare."

"And?" He said.

"It was about Julia's birthday being ruined." His light snoring came back, and I shook him awake.

"That wasn't a nightmare. I love you, but I have to work tomorrow." He fell back asleep without taking another breath.

My chest ached, and I realized what had happened. I heard the chiming of the cell phone in my eyes, and saw the pulsing of the screen. I dove out of bed, and sprinted down the stairs, only to find that the car was missing. Julie was nowhere to be found. I searched through each cupboard, expecting to find her hiding inside like when she was a kid. But she wasn't there.

The phone kept vibrating against my skull. It pulsed and pulsed, lighting up the room, until I finally saw it on the counter. A dull pink against the back countertop, vibrating, pulsing, and chiming. It wouldn't stop. I snatched it up, hoping to find the answers to every question there ever was. Instead, the screen was black and the back was missing.

Still, it was ringing. Ringing louder than ever. It sounded like a brass coin spinning on glass. I set it against my head.

"Hello?"

"Shelly." Julie's voice was distant like a desert, but

it was her. More tears sprang into my eyes.

"My little bean," I said, trying to catch my breath. I was so happy, I wanted to rip my heart from my chest.

"I finally called you." She sounded so sure of herself, so confident, like I always wanted her to be.

"I love you," I said. Tears and snot were spewing down my face. "I love you so much."

"Cool." The phone melted in my hand, and I was left with the one syllable. The "cool" brought with it a frost that coated the entire kitchen, killing the plants in the window. It made the fridge feel like a sauna. I wanted to find her. No. I needed to find her. No. I had to find her. I clutched my keys in my hand, but I couldn't convince myself to leave. Eventually, my body covered in ice and I couldn't move. My breathing became bated, and I was left staring at the phone on the ground.

Then, darkness.

CHAPTER Fourteen

"I know that you think that you may have all the answers, but I assure you that you do not. I do not. That is why we are here, in my office, now. That is why you can come to me any time when things seem to get out of hand." Dr. Howard's low voice swept past younger Dr. Wesleyan's ears. "Now, let's go over everything one more time."

Dr. Wesleyan tried not to pick at his coat, a sure tell for the other professional that he was frustrated beyond belief. He knew his boss liked to talk everyone to death. This despite having the file right in front of his aging eyes and outdated bifocals. Still, the young Dr. Wesleyan would obey the commander of the biggest desk in the facility. He would allow his affirmations to breach the wise one's ear hairs with nods of understanding. The young doctor began again with his account:

"Sixteen years ago, yesterday, Shelly, the patient, had a traumatic experience in which she lost her newlywed husband, and unborn child in a horrific car accident. She suffered traumatic brain injury. At the time, the doctor's diagnosed her with a concussion, among other major and minor bodily ailments, to include a broken hip, pelvis, and collar bone. This accident and the injuries associated resulted in a stillborn baby."

"And the baby, was it actually born?"

"Yes. Yes it was, at seven months. It didn't survive the accident but they carried out a c-section in between her other surgeries." Dr. Wesleyan watched as his mentor checked off the patient's history with a recently sharpened pencil. This was something he had seen Dr. Howard do over and over.

"And, after the incident?" Dr. Howard asked, not looking up. It was if he was checking the latest stat sheets on a sports betting paper.

"She was in a coma for nearly a year. She did not grieve for her two losses. After the coma, she did not move due to extreme psychomotor impairment. The patient entered a catatonic state that appeared to be endless. For years, the patient was replenished through intravenous means or force-fed. She did not begin to move or talk until the date which coincides with the false memory of the birth of their second child, whom she named *Andy*."

At that, Dr. Howard raised an eyebrow and tried to find that little fact on the original data sheets. It wasn't there, it was in Dr. Wesleyan's ongoing report which was in the back of the file. The young Doctor knew that, but continued with the verbal account anyway.

"At the time of the second child's *birth*, the patient began showing some progress. Her psychomotor impairment showed some signs of weakening, and she began eating and sleeping with the normal human cycle. She did not, however, have any ability to deal with reality. This derealization syndrome caused her to continue on in her mind, as if the tragedy did not occur. Her life and those of her deceased husband, daughter, and nonexistent son progressed and flourished in *real time*."

Dr. Howard winced at that last slip of the tongue. He did not like out of bounds statements or descriptions turned into less than professional slang. This briefing was not for his sake, though. He believed that if his protégé could account for all the facts of a patient, then they would have successfully established a baseline for improvement. Dr. Howard wanted to know everything that Dr. Wesleyan had absorbed, without ad lib. He stopped, though, and allowed the young man to continue.

"There were reports of extreme violence toward the staff at the last facility, Briar Hills."

At that, Dr. Howard winced further and nodded slowly with a page turn.

"I think you would agree that they had her on too many contraindicating drugs. They were testing several anti-psychotics on her at the time which may have been a cause for some ill effects."

"And now? Is she violent now?"

Dr. Wesleyan looked surprised, his boss hardly ever interrupted a briefing. He usually left all the hard questions for the end. Not sure which one he was asking, he answered, "Now I have her on strong sedatives, especially at night. She will self-harm and upend lunch trays, but she does not try to fight the orderlies. She can't have anything or she will find a way to cut herself. She came here with scars all over, some from the car accident, some from after. She has taken quite a shining to Nina Locklear, though, the day nurse, and *to me*."

Dr. Howard looked up and gave a warm smile over the desk. He showed more of his back dentures than his front teeth and Dr. Wesleyan wondered for a moment how he did that.

"You know all this. I know you watched our last session, or at least read the transcript the moment I asked for this meeting, so why make me recite it all?"

"The baseline son, the baseline." Dr. Howard sighed deep, removed his bifocals and coughed under his breath.

"What's so funny? Why are you smiling? I don't think this is funny at all," Dr. Wesleyan flicked the end of his coat over his knee.

"Oh, the youth. Yes, I can read the report and watch the videos, your sessions with the widow Mrs. Dougherty. I have even read the papers of mystery that have been written about her, or her kind. All garbage. You know why? One place claimed that her trauma to the brain made her a lost cause. Without experimental surgery, they said, she would never regain the precious reality that we all live in. That same surgery that could leave her in a coma forever. Her mother said *no* at the time and I can't blame her. She held onto hope that Shelly would recover one day and could go back home. The other facility that she spent her budding life in focused on drugs and talk therapy. The old prescription notes in her file would have even me drooling in my chair, twenty-four seven." The old Doctor stood up and slowly walked toward the window to the office that he maintained for thirty-five years. "As a younger man, I might have pushed for either."

"So, you think she's a lost cause then?"

Dr. Howard spun from the window and nearly wagged a finger. "No one is a lost cause. I gave this patient to you because you needed a challenge. You should be grateful."

"But I still don't know what to do. She thinks I'm her secret lover. That I'm some kind of disc jockey. Nina and I were the only ones there during the last episode. She's getting too close, picking up on things."

The older Doctor tilted his head and nestled his hand around his face so that his pointer finger nearly touched his graying brow. "Good," he said with some satisfying reassurance.

"How is that good? She thinks we are lovers." Dr. Wesleyan checked himself as his voice began to whine, something he knew the elder despised. He learned that from these two long years under Dr. Howard's wing. During that time, the young Doctor often dreamed of leather couches, expensive sessions, and his name on a mahogany door.

Here in this white, polished dream, reality forced itself upon him as he clocked in and out, carried clipboards, and made rounds. He was cutting his teeth and dealing with challenges he only read about in large books at school. This facility was not the first job he applied for out of residency, but it was the first one to call.

"Let her think you are lovers. She *is* restrained, right?"

"All the time or she will self-harm. Nina is the only one that can get her to eat."

"Then, take her off meds and buy into her fantasy. Be her secret lover, if only for a session."

"What?"

"You heard me. I'm the one with a hearing aid, but there's no excuse for you. Has it been tried yet?"

"No, but."

"You have interjected yourself into her world, you and Nina both. Arrange for Nina to find out about her affair with you. Arrange a meeting. She's let you in, both of you, given you a door with a key. Shelly is a riddle with no answer. This young woman, this precious life, has been thrust upon us. She represents an opportunity. Will she ever drive a car or buy groceries or go back to college? Not likely. The only item of significance that we can offer her is hope. It is likely that she doesn't want to do any of those things anyway. In that respect, I can agree with the previous Doctors' analyses. She *is* beyond repair. Yet, she is not without *hope*. She *hopes* for a better future in her world, in her reality. She *hopes* to be a better businesswoman, a better mother, a better wife. She rattles on all day with clues, just for you and Nina, on how to break into her world and give her that *real* hope."

"But, I will be giving her false hope. I will be buying into her fantasy. Is that not *cruel*?"

"Cruel is leaving her sedated. Cruel is cutting into her brain and hoping for the best. We must leave her restrained, for her protection, *and* your own. But that does not mean we can't go to her level. Trust me, if you can meet her where she sits, you will get a better reaction. You know that psychosis of this level goes beyond an overactive dopamine system. You know your limits. Go beyond them. I will make sure that in your next session, the video feed will be off. Nina can be there with you, but you must at least try."

"Try what?"

"Don't be coy. Now is not the time. Mrs. Dougherty has been through a terrible tragedy. She lost her husband and her baby. In one automobile accident, she also lost her mind. But more than that, she lost *hope*. Give her hope outside her normal world. She has given you a door and I am telling you to go across the threshold. Seize this opportunity, and your career will be made *for you*."

Dr. Wesleyan noticed that his protégé session and pep talk was over. He stood to leave, trying to contain his own panic.

CHAPTER Fifteen

"Oh, Wesley wants to see me! Oh, he sent you! How smart, he must know it will be safer that way. I should fix my hair. Can you help me fix my hair? Do you have any of that peach lipstick? I want him to think of me when he sees it. I want Wesley to taste that flavor on my lips. No, you wouldn't carry it around, not for this, not for me. How much time do I have to get ready?"

"No dear, we don't have any lipstick here." Nina calmly began to change the patient's bland gown and put on the jacket. The buckles hardly made a sound. Years of experience silenced them.

"Oh, how much time do I have to get ready?"

"No time to waste dear, he's ready for you now."

"But I haven't seen him since the party. I hope he's

not mad at me. Is Wesley mad at me? Could you tell from his voice, from his tone? Did I break anything of his?"

"No, I don't think he's mad at you, but he is excited to see you. We must go."

"I have just the thing to tell him too. I have a *secret*."

"What secret dear?"

"I don't know if I should...Well, you already know but...I don't know if I should te- I don't know if I should tell you. Oh, you'll be so upset with me."

"What's that now?" The ward asked, only stopping her practiced motions of restraint for a subtle moment.

"Is this my gown? Oh, you're right, I should wear this dress. He likes it when I wear this dress."

"Yes, he does, you have to wear nice clothes when you see him. *I'm* used to seeing you the other way, but..."

"Oh, he loves this dress. Do I have to wear the shawl too?"

"Yes dear, it's cold in his apartment. We'll have to bundle up, remember?"

"But...you don't have to...It doesn't have to be so tight, does it?"

"You'll be fine dear, I'll make sure. I won't put it too tight."

"You're right, this shawl is very warm and cozy. So

warm, hot almost. Hot like his storage unit."

"Well, they fixed the air dear, so it won't be so hot in there for you. Come along then, let's stand up. Let me just tie this here so you're not showing off. There. Are you ready then?"

"Oh I know, he likes to take off my clothes. You should see the way he handles me. The way he ravished me earlier, oh you wouldn't believe. Nina, are you blushing yet? I'm sorry, but I have to tell somebody, I have to…"

"It's fine dear, you can tell me. I won't tell anybody else. Your secret is safe. Come along now."

"But I just…I want to make sure I look good. Do you have your compact?"

"No, I don't have my compact with me. Must have left it in the car. But I can tell you look marvelous. Now, if we could just…"

"But, before I see him again, I have to put something by you. I have to tell you *a secret*."

"Dear, I already told you that you could."

"I think I'm pregnant."

"What?" Nina stopped trying to get Shelly past the door of her cell.

"That's it. I think I'm pregnant and I think it's his baby. I *know* it's his baby. I can *feel* that it's *his*. He

141

wanted me. I took him. I took all his power. I made *him* do those things. And he *gave me* something. It's all mine now. He won't have a word to say about it. I might not tell him. I might just...let the secret linger inside of me for a while, until I'm sure. But it's his, I can *feel* that it's *his*. I want it to be *his*. I can tell you, right? I don't want to tell anybody else, but I can tell *you*. *I'm having his baby*."

"Um...alright dear. I'm your friend and you've told me. Good, that's good." Nina, ever stoic in white, began to lose control but tried to play along with her *best friend*.

"Do you think he'll want me still? Men are like that sometimes. They don't want you once you...once you start to show fat. Once your little belly pushes out like this. Oh, I can't get it out with the shawl but, well, you know. Maybe you could tell him. Maybe you *should* tell him in *your* way, the way you tell *me* things. If I *say* it's alright for you to tell *him*, then you're still keeping the secret, right? As long as you don't tell *Andrew*. Andrew can't know. Andrew got snipped after our second child. I was going to get my tubes tied but then, *he offered*. I'm glad, too. Andrew deserved it. Not that he really did anything, not like me. I just didn't want him to have more babies. I didn't want to have any more babies either, but *just in case*. Oh, maybe you *should* tell him. I don't know what he'll do. Should I just wait? Will he want a paternity test? Will we be on one of those shows where they reveal *who the father is*? Oh, I can't do that to Andrew. And the kids! Wow, they'll have a brother or sister! I just won't tell anybody but you, that's it. But maybe you can give him a hint is all. Maybe you could just make him think I'm special, if he doesn't already *know*."

"Alright dear, I won't say anything, and *you* won't say anything either. We'll just leave it at that, but we have to be going now. He is waiting for you. He wants to see you. *Wesley* has called on you and wanted me to come find you... so *Andrew* wouldn't know."

"Yeah, so Andrew wouldn't know. So smart. So wicked. Such a hunk. Do I look good? I mean, really?"

Yes, you look fine dear, now come along."

The pair in white made a sound so vague as they walked down the hall that unless a person, or a camera, saw one assisting the other, there would be no telling the difference between the two real souls and a pair of tangled apparitions. The ward let go of her patient only to open one corridor's lock. They shuffled through one, then another.

She led the mumbling child into an empty room with a voice box recorder molded into the bleached-white desk. There was no mirrored glass wall which belonged in plenty of other rooms. There was a camera though, mounted in the upper right-hand corner. The eye peered down at the question and answer playground for the insane. The air remained stuck in time. No slight breeze penetrated the thick, concrete walls, or barred and cloudy window. No circulation from whispering vents or tunnels of escape.

There was a confused, small, midday light that shone through the opaque glass. It penetrated without motive. The flourescent tubes from above came to life from the motion of nurse and patient. A best friend with a secret tended to her child like a stern mother with painstaking attention and sense of duty.

Nina's own feminine virtues were not lost in the uniform. She remained tight and kept as she tidied her bundle of blind innocence. Nina tucked fabric here and there, adjusting the jacket, for both comfort and safety. Her patient rarely wore clothes. Shelly preferred easy access to the clawing and gnawing of her own flesh. To the fascination of blood running down her legs. Shelly was usually found in the bedding of ripped strips, always along the white on white stripes with red stains of joy, and always before breakfast.

There was no doubt that the nurse cared. She was there to care. So much that an onlooker might wonder how the mother in white would spend her free time after clocking out. After the next row of girls and women would come to call with their uniforms and starch, it was hard to imagine what would be next in the day for someone like Nina. There were smells that offended certain patients, so the wards were made void of such pleasures as candy lip balm or perfume. Without makeup or feminine pleasantries, the nurses played statue or nun pretty. Not so playful, not so kind, but always with a purpose.

As Nina made final adjustments and clipped the patient to the floor, Shelly cooed herself to sleep over secrets and excitement, sensual desire and touch. Her lack of medication kept her up all hours, which meant nodding off and giggling to herself during the day, forever dreaming.

Nina looked at her patient and recognized the peace and tranquility. She gave her thumbs up to the corner eye. She knew he would be watching. He wanted the all clear this time.

It was during the last session that the patient became violent in a strange, sexual manner. Shelly had revealed how she felt for the Doctor, or, how she thought she felt for the disc jockey of her daughter's sweet sixteen. During the last session, she was not clipped in and had tried to kiss him, bite him, with sensual desire, and demanded reciprocation.

She had chased him around the small, hot room whose airflow was neglected to the changing season. Last time, Shelly thrust her womanhood on Dr. Wesleyan and broke his chair on the light above. This also broke his will. He didn't know what to do and had screamed into the intercom as she licked the back of his neck. She had stretched and pulled off the bottom of her gown and flung it off at her prey.

She was pulled off and abruptly medicated after she was found by the orderlies thrusting her body wildly over the frightened Doctor, pinning him to the corner with her hot breath and moans.

Dr. Wesleyan did try and avoid her previous advances and her flirtations. It threw him off guard, but her smell of wanting and the brightness in her eyes when she saw him made him play along at times. He tried to enter her world.

It wasn't the flicker in her eyes, not really, but the ritual look about her pupils that called for playful advancement. The wanting. She was beautiful somewhere behind the scars and he wanted nothing more than for her to come back to life.

He believed that it had gone too far during previous sessions even, before he had screamed into the intercom like a sad puppy who scratched at the door. She pinned him to that corner, but he had the notion that he put himself there, had asked for it. That part, he didn't tell his boss. Perhaps the old man already knew.

Dr. Wesleyan wanted nothing more than the pleasure of talking to someone he knew was in there. Someone in pain, someone who needed him. Not the person who he tried to train to eat and not bludgeon herself for the last eighteen months, but someone real, someone partly sane.

Their *relationship* was a cable. A snap of metal

drawn so tight around a theatre of the strange. The Doctor never thought a patient could be so volatile, could get under his skin, into his life. He had dealt with murderers, even rapists in his residency. They maintained their distance. He figured he helped. He played his role; a man with authority and power who loomed over them.

But this one, this one believed something different.

The Doctor entered and motioned for the nurse to stay which she took for a sign to leave. Their discourse was awkward at best, his nervous tension shuddered through his white coat. The nurse understood his face and waited by the door with a keen eye. She was ready to conduct banishment of her confused, feline child in heat, should the need arise.

"I'm pregnant, and it's yours Wesley," Shelly declared, snapping to. Her glowing eyes beamed with joy at the Doctor.

"How are you feeling today, Shelly?" Dr. Wesleyan cleared his throat and tried to ignore the declaration of child.

"I'm doing well. Well done. The baby is real, I can feel him talking through my belly button." Shelly began rocking in her seat again, but instead of looking wildly around the room or staring into the table, she beamed at the Doctor with the freshness and rosy cheeks of a woman with child. She rubbed her stomach through the jacket. This made him nervous.

"And what does the baby say?" Dr. Wesleyan asked.

Shelly began to rock harder and pecked with her eyes again about the room, "Telling me to rip the wings off of butterflies. He told me that I had an accident. I'd remember *that* if I did. I would, wouldn't I? I think I would remember doing that. He told me I had a quieting inside. Such a big imagination. Julie? She's back at the house."

"Julie is back at the house? What is Julie doing now?"

"I can hear every time her phone rings. Rinnng. Riiiing. Riiiiiiiinnnnnng. It pierces through my head, burrows in there, nesting. That phone is always there. I'm trapped behind the glass, tapped, tap, tapping, looking at the baby. Hanging from the ceiling by his umbilical cord. Sometimes when I look out the window, I see the birds. The birds are waiting to blind me, they don't want me to see Andrew. They want me to know the truth of our love, but the baby isn't like that. The baby knows exactly what I should know."

"What does the baby know?"

"*Our* baby is an angel speaking to me in my dreams, telling me where the sharp objects are in my office." She beamed at him again. "The sharpest thing is a chipped piece of porcelain. It's a stained link in a chain- from all the blood, a beautiful pink color. Accidents can't be real, because I saw *everyone* just yesterday."

"Who did you see yesterday?" the Doctor asked.

"Nina? She's my best friend. Wes, before I met you, I was ready to take my life. My entire world. Plastic flamingos and fake lawn ornaments pretending to be something...no. They're just standing there, pretending, pretending to be... real birds. No, real birds stay outside windows, talking to you. Our baby... I want you to stay with me forever."

"What are you pretending Shelly?"

Her eyes locked with his and she seemed offended by the question. "I want to eat your skin and bones and keep you inside of me like the baby. You can sleep there and hold him before he is born. And I could feel both of your breaths through my mouth. I could taste the love and joy you both give off."

She tried to stand and come after him again, the Doctor flinched a little.

"I..."

She cut him off with her continued declaration and her voice heightened over the buzz of the bright lights. "Radiating like a sun of blood and flesh and joy. I want you to clutch me from the inside. When I sleep, I can almost feel you caressing my bare skin with your finger, playing me like a violin. You always play a sad song, our song, the baby's song. It's the same song we made love to, the one that was playing. I can hum it for you, if you don't remember." She began to hum something incoherent and breathy.

"That is a nice song Shelly. Yes, I do like that song...*our* song." Dr. Wesleyan fought every urge not to play along. He felt it wrong but wanted to take the advice, the big pill, fulfill the experiment. He sat up in his chair and tried to retain his composure. "What about the accident? Can you tell me about that?"

"The accident is still there but I don't know. Don't know. Burning and screaming. The plastic flamingos screaming, holding their melty faces. It's not there. Why do they need their human faces? They don't need them. I tear them away. Try to stop the screaming but the fake pink melting. Coo. Coo. Coo. Coo. Coo. Red and blue and white owls, screeching bright light. Bright, terrible lights, and fire that eats rooms and my eyes. My eyes melt from the light, and I can't breathe. Have I ever? Yes. Am I able to breathe? Yes."

"You're breathing just fine Shelly, but you have to calm down so we can talk. So we can spend time together and talk about...*our baby*." The words made him sick. He didn't like to lie. Ever since he told his mom that his cousin broke the window and she found out the truth. Lying made him feel dirty, unworthy of the coat, and the responsibility.

"The baby says that I could breathe before the accident. I won't have another one, because I've never had one. He says there are white eyes, lump of flesh, nobody's heartbeat. No, but this baby will be a lumberjack with a beard and an ax, and he'll chop down trees to make way for his mom. I'm going to live in a log cabin with him. You can come, if it's okay. We can have a secret getaway. I'll find the land in a secret listing only for realtors. Andrew won't know."

"Yes, I would like that very much, but tell me more about the accident."

"I know you have your music. I'll be your instrument, if you need one. I know you'll be happy playing me. Finger my strings, and beat my ivories, and blow my brass, whatever works best. I want you to hold me, can't you hold me now? Why are you being so cold? I know you are surprised, I am too. I make a good wife. You don't have to marry me though, I still have Andrew. He doesn't know, does he? No, he can't know, he's not here. He won't know about us. Nina won't tell. I'd make a good wife, but an even better, *secret lover*." She smiled, even giggled with delight, but the pain returned.

"That's fine Shelly, and you're right, Andrew isn't here, it's just us. We can be together. But we have to talk about the accident." Dr. Wesleyan choked on his own words.

"I'm not happy unless I'm with you. You make the butterflies in my skin cool down and the birds stay away from the window. Why would the baby say such awful things? Why would the baby tell me such nonsense? I've never been in an accident. Why would the baby lie?! Have you been lying to me? Did you put lying sperm into my egg? You *are* such a salty lover. If I'm not a liar, you must be."

"No one is lying to you here," Dr. Wesleyan felt the pain of the switch and broken glass on a summer evening. This was one of the few times that he hated his dream.

"I hate you! Touch me! Love me! Why don't you hold me anymore? You keep your love and your warmth. Mother hen? Mother hen, where are you?" Her eyes darted around the room, then back at the Doctor. "You warm my heart and all I do is bleed for you. I do it for you! Don't you see? Don't you want me? You wanted me before, before the party, and I knew. Hold me Wes! Don't you love me? Aren't I beautiful to you anymore?" She tested the restraints and wept as she moaned sadness to her lover.

"You have to calm down Shelly, or…" he stammered but couldn't tell her he was going to leave. He wanted to stand up and hold her, tell her it was going to be alright, everything would be fine. He imagined her cold, sunless skin against his. He desired to feel her hair tickle his arm as her tears melt into his jacket.

If he held her as Wes would, comforted her and the baby inside, she might cry herself out. If he let her go from the restraints and just clutched her body as her forbidden lover, she could be in the here, in the now. She could be free from dead Andrew and the stillborn Julia. She could put her mindless wanderings on the future, *their* future.

The tradeoff was too much to bear. Dr. Wesleyan's legs and chest became frozen. He stared at Shelly. She was a delicate pile of pain. She was sobbing. His heart froze over, numbed to the possibilities of love. He reacted to his own sadness, for the regret of a missed chance at life and happiness. The father of her child, yet another figment. If he just stood and held her, he could be real.

A tear formed in the corner of his eye and slid down his cheek. This never happened, not here. Only alone at night. Only in the dark of the empty sheets, the sadness of a thousand stories took him. He never told anyone. He wept alone to his pillow with no one watching, no one to conduct an analysis. All their horrible acts, all their illusions, all their missed lives crept in on him in the darkness. They swept over his whispers in the dull void before his own dreams and illusions could take over. He never told anyone. Too strong, too legit, too successful, too here.

They were creeping in now as he watched her with nothing left to say. *Hold her! Hold her!* His mind cried out to his capable, yet unwilling hands.

Before a second tear could form, he stood up and turned his back. As he unhinged the bolt, he heard Shelly wail, thrash, and scream for her lover.

Those sounds were real.

Alone. I was alone. No. Because I was never alone now. I had the baby inside of me. The baby loved me and wanted to talk to me. The baby would tell me stories and hold me from inside, even if Wesley wanted nothing to do with him. I could feel the baby wrap his arms around my womb, holding me, cooing softly to me. Wearing my intestines like a scarf.

I love you. He was too busy hugging and cooing to respond. The baby pulled from his hug, and I felt the searing sensation race across my veins. It flickered down the length of my arm, revealing the long black bones below my skin that were held together by long, dark screws. I screeched into the sky, unable to catch my breath. The terrible sound burst the bulb above my head, and the darkness dropped from the ceiling, pooling on the floor.

Another burst of pain radiated down my spine, racing towards the baby. The hot butterflies filled my womb, crashing, smashing him against my walls of skin. The baby thrashed in my womb kicking at my cervix, trying to get free. A cool burst pushed over my body, and the pain stopped. In that moment, I stopped to gather my breath in my lungs.

Breathe. Breathe. Breathe. Then, another burst of

pain shot through my body. Breathe. Breathe. Another shot of pain forced through me again. The baby was trying to find his way out.

The darkness on the ground had since morphed and shaped itself into Andrew, Andy, and Julie. Their black feathers were sleeker than I remembered, and their beaks sharper, and their eyes beadier, but their faces were nice and smooth. Blemish free. They were looking their best to come see me give birth.

Bright white lights flickered down my legs, feeding my nerves pain. Pain I didn't want. I wanted to be free of my skin. Free of my pain. I'd rip it off. The baby had said that I could, and I would. The dual lights pulsed away from my body and hit Andrew. I smiled at him, glad that he would take some of the pain away.

Thank you. He tilted his feathered head to look at my half smile, and his head fell away from his body. It rolled back into the darkness as the emptiness swallowed.

A roar like thunder radiated from the ceiling, as more darkness slipped its tendrils towards me. I tried to focus on the thunder, but the more I attempted to focus, the more it shifted. What I had thought sounded like thunder began sounding like the roar of a train. No, a lion's roar.

The dangling darkness hung down to my body, holding me in place to face the ceiling. It pressed into my bulging stomach, and slit me open from ribs to pelvis.

The darkness cracked me open like an egg, pouring the white-hot butterflies onto the floor. They moved forward, gripping ahold of Julie, burning her instead of me. She was nothing but ash.

The shadows punched into my belly. They wrapped around my insides, and yanked on them. Torn out. Another tug. Another. Another. Yolk out of my womb.

The baby was dripping blood onto my chest in heart patterns. Dripping. Dripping love onto my chest. The darkness coated over Andy, pulling him into the deep. The baby was how I imagined he would be.

A lump of pink flesh. A lump of my flesh, shapeless like dough, ready to be molded into anything. I wanted to teach him, but before I could, the pain flickered under my skin. The butterflies, the first, they were coming back for him. I hugged my baby against my chest, and pushed him back into my body.

I'll keep you safe inside until I can cut their wings. When everything was safe again. With one hand, I crimped the two sides of my big cut, keeping the baby fresh inside of me. Nothing was going to take him away. Nothing.

The blood from my body coated my hands like red colored gloves. My blood, Wesley's blood. It coated my body along the edges. My body was less a vessel. My rib cage provided bars for my son to hide behind. They were not a prison. Not a prison.

No, the bars were for him. The bars were for the baby. Like bars on a crib. They held him tight and held him close. Crib. I wanted to rush up and tell Wesley, but he had already gone. He had already wandered away into the nothing. Into the abyss. And I was trapped, clutching a baby in my chest, hoping the darkness would dissipate.

Not even the jaws of an alligator could crush my strength. My strength. The baby nestled against my heart, holding it like an egg, pressing it to his own. This was how we would survive, I would keep him safe and he would keep me.

The darkness contorted and shaped. A broken piece of porcelain. Cut porcelain stained pink floated down like a feather to my hand.

The answer was obvious. I pressed the porcelain into my skin and ran it along my flesh like a zipper. Opening myself up to grab the baby. Like the porcelain, he was stained pink. Cracked, but beautiful.

The deep red placenta dripped onto the floor. Drip. Drip. Drip. Drip. My baby to hold and squeeze. His face was a round tomato, perfect. The butterflies flickered on the wall, forming into two giant spheres, shining light into my eyes. A constant reminder of pain. They were leaving.

My energy drained away in waves. I needed sleep. When I would wake up, I could find Wesley and prove to him I wasn't lying. I could cut him and let his butterflies free into the sky.

No one needed pain. No one. I could show Wesley that our son was with us now.

CHAPTER Sixteen

The crisp morning of early spring was begging for a stay on the thermostats all throughout the facility. The damp air warned of winter forging on and its spirit shown itself on the visible breaths of those who dared venture before the sun could take over. Cut off by midday, the cold showed itself one last time after breakfast.

The grounds were expertly enclosed for safety. But the mixture of trees, peeking bulbs, and benches for spying on birds, gave the outside a warm feeling of being lost. A forest green and brown contrast to the harsh whites and the all-seeing eyes on the inside led some to take their walks or do their reading. All accompanied of course.

After breakfast. The term gave new meaning to Shelly as spring arrived. A new routine to follow, something to look forward to.

After breakfast. Every day. Except Sundays, she and Andrew would still take Andy to church, and Julie, if she would wake up in time. All other six days, she would make an excuse if she needed. Some days, she would make her little excuses to no one.

Nina usually helped her get to the park with the nice benches for sitting, and the nice birds to hear chirping. Shelly knew her son liked it there, with all the sounds and the clean air. He smiled when they went as his eyes gazed at all the new sights, all the wonderful songs to be heard. She named him Daniel, after her grandfather. Daniel was eating well, sleeping well, and giving Shelly such great joy and purpose.

He was a good baby, but the pregnancy had taken its toll on Shelly. That is why Nina had accompanied her on most outdoor retreats. Nina was there that day, and had just wiped a nice bench clean with a white towel after a nearby automatic sprinkler had just completed its song for the surrounding grass along the edge of the trail. Nina stood guard and folded the towel with precision over her arm. She was so attentive, so caring. *Such a good friend.*

"I know you love it out here, don't you Daniel? What a nice day, crisp even. Are you warm enough? Yes, you'll be fine, right here all folded up with me." Shelly cooed at the bundle of joy in her arms while Nina remained stoic. "Nina? Do you think he looks flush today? He ate so much last night and this morning. Does he look like he's growing to you?" Shelly asked.

"He looks fine dear, and yes, he is growing up quite fast," Nina didn't need practice, she answered the same every day. She was, however, happy regarding the recent events which led Shelly to spend more time outside, instead of always cooped up. Nina's *friend* had also stopped harming herself since the newborn. Instead, Shelly dedicated her idle hours to changing diapers and breastfeeding.

"What about your babies, Nina? Did *they* all grow fast?"

"Oh, like weeds Shelly, like weeds they did."

"You hear that Daniel? You've got some competition, *yes you do...*"

Just then, a patch of footwork sounded down the path and a white coat swayed in the distance with a marching clipboard and tie.

"He's on his way then?" Shelly asked without looking.

"Yes dear, he is," Nina answered, turning her head in the direction of the Doctor.

"Oh, I'm so glad my Wes could make it today. He is so dependable. You hear that Daniel? *Daddy's coming to see you.*"

"Hello dear, how are we feeling today?" Dr. Wesleyan paused in front of Shelly on the bench and gave a real smile with the knowing question. It was nice to see her in another setting besides that room. That room where he made those mistakes, where he almost got hurt. He drew in a dramatic breath of fresh air, looked around for a moment, and said, "What a lovely day."

"Yes it is dear, so nice to see you, and *we* are doing splendid." With the last word, Shelly looked down at Daniel, then back up at Wes with an expectant turn of her cheek.

The Doctor gave a nervous look around for a moment, then one glare at Nina who answered with a marbled expression. He slid one hand behind Shelly's shoulder blade, leaned down, and gave her a heartfelt peck on her cheek. As he remained near the warmth of her face, he took a good look at their bundle and said, "My! Did he grow up overnight? So big! He'll be rounding third in no time at the ball fields. Isn't that right, Daniel?"

Shelly giggled, the way she only did when Wes talked to Daniel directly. Happiness blew out her cheeks and made dimples. Then, she composed herself and clenched the child tighter, as she did every time she attempted the uneasy question, "Would you like to hold him today?" She held her breath as her eyes called to Wes to meet hers before tears could well.

The Doctor could not bear to see her cry again, not this morning. She had made too much progress. He glanced at Nina, who again offered nothing in return but hard truths behind her statue demeanor. He caved a little, hardened again, then caught Shelly's expectant eyes. He refused to be the reason for those tears today.

"Sure dear, but let's walk a little too. That way, you can point out all the birds."

Wes held out his hands and felt the new weight of the growing baby on his forearms, then he carefully patted the little head to his shoulder.

The four took in the majesty of early spring, and continued down the path.

MARC D. CREPEAUX & A.M. HOUNCHELL

Marc D. Crepeaux is a curator, editor and writer for the *Letters Never Meant to be Read* series. Marc has also authored the gritty, Southern crime novel *Modern Waste*, the poetry collection *Worked Stiff: Poetry and Prose for the Common* along with the collection's sequel *Worked Stiff: Short Stories to Tell Your Boss*. He is from Killawog, NY and spent much of his late-teens and early twenties in NYC where he acted like a maniac. He now works as an English professor and a Captain in the Army Reserves, among other entrepreneurial endeavors. He holds an MFA in Creative Writing. Marc lives in a more calming environment with his wife, three daughters, two dogs, two goats, and one Russian tortoise in an old farmhouse right around Rome, GA. He can be found in excess on marcdcrepeaux.com and lettersandbooks.com

A.M. Hounchell is a recent college graduate and newlywed. His claim to fame is *Contractual Obligations*, a novel with choices, and *Running Out of Time*, his unedited and absurd novel. Houchell has also penned and edited pure force to the *Letters Never Meant to be Read* series. He has two cats, Swarley and Kiwi. Currently, he lives in Kansas with his beautiful wife, Grace. He can be found on amhounchell.ninja

If You've Enjoyed this Book, Please Check Out These Other Titles from the Catalog of Rusty Wheels Media, LLC.

or visit lettersandbooks.com

In the Mist of Fire by Nathalie Gribinski

Stop That Wedding

Quintessential Reality

Letters Never Meant to be Read (Volume III)

Letters Never Meant to be Read (Volume II)

Letters Never Meant to be Read (Volume I)

Contractual Obligations

Worked Stiff: Poetry and Prose for the Common

Worked Stiff: Short Stories to Tell Your Boss

Where Did You Go?: A 21st Century Guide to Finding Yourself Again

The Forge: Certified Six Sigma Green Belt Certification Program Workbook

QUINTESSENTIAL REALITY

As Always,

If you have any letters, books, or poetry of your own, send them to us, manuscripts will always be considered for the collection…

editor@lettersandbooks.com

or

Rusty Wheels Media, LLC

PO Box 1692

Rome, GA 30162

Lettersandbooks.com

Made in the USA
Columbia, SC
08 December 2018